A Candlelight Ecstasy Romance ®

"YOU DON'T BELIEVE IN LOVE AT FIRST SIGHT?"

"No."

"How long should it take to fall in love?" Bram rested his chin on her shoulder.

"Look, if you're perfectly honest, you'll admit you're not in love. I'm sure that by the time morning comes you'll see that this was just a slight case of temporary insanity."

Bram yawned. "Who knows"—he kept his tone light—"you could be right." He yawned again and pulled the coverlet around his shoulders.

She punched a pillow into softness before her head landed on it. *Of course I'm right,* Roxanne silently declared. *You don't fall in love in two days. It's just not possible. Even if it were, even if I did, I would fight against it. I don't need to fall in love with any man—especially Bram Tyler.*

CANDLELIGHT ECSTASY ROMANCES ®

SPECIAL DELIVERY

Elaine Raco Chase

A CANDLELIGHT ECSTASY ROMANCE®

Published by
Dell Publishing Co., Inc.
1 Dag Hammarskjold Plaza
New York, New York 10017

Dell ® TM 681510, Dell Publishing Co., Inc.

Candlelight Ecstasy Romance®, 1,203,540, is a registered
trademark of Dell Publishing Co., Inc., New York, New York.

ISBN: 0–440–18164–X

Printed in the United States of America

First printing—April 1984

I'd like to thank the following people for their help in making this book possible:

Minneapolis Romance Author LaVyrle Spencer for sending me all sorts of information on her wonderful city and putting me in touch with:

Carolyn Healey, Director of Communications, Greater Minneapolis Chamber of Commerce . . .

Carolyn Pace, Customer Relations, Shell Oil Company, for helping me remember how to drive on snow . . .

Claudia Huber, Daytona Beach, for her knowledge of banking . . .

NOAA—National Oceanic and Atmospheric Administration—for their help in creating a blizzard . . .

and last but never least, to Anne Gisonny, my very tolerant, patient, and wonderfully supportive editor, who waited so long she forgot about this hopefully Special Delivery

To Our Readers:

We have been delighted with your enthusiastic response to Candlelight Ecstasy Romances®, and we thank you for the interest you have shown in this exciting series.

In the upcoming months we will continue to present the distinctive sensuous love stories you have come to expect only from Ecstasy. We look forward to bringing you many more books from your favorite authors and also the very finest work from new authors of contemporary romantic fiction.

As always, we are striving to present the unique, absorbing love stories that you enjoy most—books that are more than ordinary romance.

Your suggestions and comments are always welcome. Please write to us at the address below.

Sincerely,

The Editors
Candlelight Romances
1 Dag Hammarskjold Plaza
New York, New York 10017

CHAPTER ONE

When the telephone beeped five minutes before closing time on Friday, Roxanne hesitated only a fraction of a second before lifting the receiver. "Greetings and salutations, how may I help you?" Her husky contralto bid an engaging welcome across the line.

"Miss . . . Miss Murdoch this is Leah, Leah Chang. Oh, I'm so sorry about this. I . . . I just get this job with you and now . . . now I—I've made such a mess of everything. Please . . . please give me another chance?" The young woman's words were a jumbled, rapid staccato.

Slender fingers tightened their grip on the red phone. "Calm down, Leah," Roxanne ordered, her voice matching her directive. Three vertical lines interrupted the smoothness of her forehead as she tried to decipher the unusual background noises. "Where are you?"

"University Hospital. The emergency room," she answered, ever-increasing sniffles punctuating each statement. Then Roxanne heard her pull the receiver away. "Will you please wait a minute, I'm talking with my boss. Don't you think I know the damn thing's broken!"

"What did you break, Leah?"

"Well, Miss Murdoch, at the moment it feels like everything," the University of Minnesota student sniffled again, then hiccuped, "but according to the X rays it's my left arm and my right ankle."

Roxanne winced. Despite the warm air blowing from the heat registers of the wooden floor, a sudden chill transversed her spine, making her shoulders bunch beneath the double-breasted gray flannel suit jacket. "How on earth did that happen?"

"It's snowing and icy and I lost my footing while I was trying to board the bus to come to work," Leah grumbled. "My own fault. I was late and I was running and not wearing boots and now—"

"Do you need your employee's group insurance number?" her boss inquired, fingers immediately twisting the black knob on the Rolodex to the letter I.

"No. No. That's not the problem, that's not why I called. Miss Murdoch, I'm supposed to deliver a message at six o'clock, only I'll be wearing plaster of Paris instead of—" The young woman's voice again turned away to argue with someone else.

"Leah! Leah!" Roxanne managed to regain her employee's attention. "Don't worry. I'll find someone else to deliver it. You just cooperate with the doctor and relax. Your job will be waiting for you."

She smiled at the responding sigh of relief. "What about transportation back to your dorm?"

"I called my boyfriend. Todd's coming for me. We were going to ski in the New Year this weekend but now . . ." Her teariness had returned, accompanied by a symphony of hiccups. "They're wheeling me away. I'm really sorry about this, Miss Murdoch. I—I should have been more carefullll." The last syllable of the word faded into the distance and became permanently terminated by the dial tone.

Roxanne eyed the schoolroom-style clock over the office door. She had an hour to go until six but only thirty minutes at the most to find a replacement for Leah Chang. Her capable fingers stroked through the plump telephone index file before moving to press in the numbers of the Beta House sorority. Eight long rings later someone finally answered. "I'd like to speak to Suzy Lewis."

"Sorry, she went to Florida for the holidays."

"How about Debbie Capshaw?" came Roxanne's hopeful inquiry.

"According to this list posted on the bulletin board, she's at Squaw Valley."

Clear-glossed nails tapdanced over the desk's scratched wooden surface while Roxanne inquired after ten other students. She was chagrined to discover her regular stable of student employees had departed the Twin Cities in search of either Southern sun or a winter skiing wonderland.

"This is Christmas vacation, lady, four days before New Year's," the woman grated in annoyance. "You're lucky I even picked up this phone. I'm only

13

hired to clean up the mess these girls leave, not to be their answering service."

Once again Roxanne Murdoch found her ear assaulted by a rude bang and serenaded with a monotone hum. "Let's advance to alternate plan B," she murmured, and starting at the beginning of the alphabet called the various theater groups whose members she had often hired.

After encountering a succession of unanswered telephones and the end of her Rolodex, Roxanne acknowledged the futility of her efforts. The last week of the year seemed to be the least inhabited one in Minneapolis. Alert brown eyes watched the hands on the clock persistently click away precious minutes before shifting to stare at the framed poster on the pseudo-hickory paneled wall.

A cuddly looking King Kong–size gorilla with a smiling clown clutched in one monster hand and pastel balloons in the other grinned at Roxanne. The printed copy read: *When you want to send a memorable message, call Greetings and Salutations. Select from over one hundred original, professional, funny musical performances. We guarantee to deliver anything the law allows—twenty-four hours a day, three hundred sixty-five days a year!*

The word *guarantee* bloated to gigantic proportions in Roxanne's mind. The smile that curved her full lips was reciprocated in her eyes. In the four years since she had become a successful entrepreneur and started Greetings and Salutations, the guarantee had never been forfeited. Why, her company was more dependable than the U. S. mail—neither rain nor snow nor sleet nor hail . . . and she wasn't about to default now.

Palms flattened on the desktop, Roxanne pushed herself out of the red posture chair. "Emergency alternative now in effect." Her audible mandate fell on the shoulders of the only person populating the small back office—herself!

True, she hadn't personally delivered a message in over two years. But in the beginning, during those lean days that were riddled with doubts and misgivings, Roxanne had sung her way through hundreds of balloon-o-grams, danced and juggled greetings as a clown, and lumbered through many a restaurant as a gorilla in a tuxedo. She had been a leprechaun, an Easter bunny, a fairy godmother, a dancing birthday cake, and ninety percent of the Disney cartoon characters.

All it took was a positive attitude, a hefty dose of self-confidence, and a thick skin, to succeed and overcome the risk of failure and initial feelings of embarrassment. Every message was delivered with an attitude of good, clean fun; nothing tasteless or illegal. Her ethical standards were high, and the greetings were certainly more remembered than any store-bought card.

Business had boomed courtesy of a newspaper feature article, a local TV interview program, word of mouth, and some creative advertising. Despite the fluctuating economy, it seemed people were more than willing to let Greetings and Salutations fill their need for fun. Roxanne had become the consummate executive. She spent her time creating new messages

and skits, designing costumes, recording clever telephone-answering cassettes, and was now working on
franchising her concepts. These days college students, local actors and actresses, and commercial
models fulfilled the message demands.

Conscious of the hour, Roxanne strode across the
room to the hanging visible card file. She flipped
through the plastic-covered pages, reacquainting
herself with the bookings that had transpired while
she had been enjoying Christmas with her family in
Chicago. A frown marred her features: Major holidays were notoriously barren, and this had been no
exception. She was thankful that the weeks ahead
were already accumulating more stellar business
than this disappointing roster.

On Monday a single balloon birthday greeting had
been logged, nothing Tuesday or Wednesday, and
yesterday another balloon-o-gram had been delivered. Birthday greetings seemed to be the order of
this marginal week. Roxanne's voice limbered
through the musical scales, warming up to sing
"Happy Birthday" while dressed in an old-fashioned
Western Union messenger suit.

The dulcet tones of the birthday song strangled in
her throat as she discovered Leah Chang's Greeting
and Salutation assignment was a belly-gram! Roxanne's eyelids squeezed tightly shut, then opened
wide, hoping that the inked instructions would magi-
cally transpose themselves into something else. They
didn't.

She pulled the oversize file card from its protective
shield and read the notation. Sender: six senior vice

presidents at the Hepworth National Bank. Receiver: Abraham L. Tyler, the newly appointed senior vice president in charge of commercial loans. Request: belly dancer—dance of the seven veils for congratulations on his promotion to seventh senior V.P.

Despite her initial shock, Roxanne couldn't stifle her laughter. "And who said bankers wore stuffed shirts beneath their three-piece Brooks Brothers suits!" came her crowing statement. "Those little rascals! Poor old Abe Tyler." Her mind's eye pictured a stoop-shouldered, nearly bald octogenarian holding a stovepipe hat. "After this congratulations greeting he'll ring in the New Year in the coronary care unit!"

"Belly dancer, hmm." She tapped the card against her chin. This was a relatively new greeting she had added due to frequent client requests. The bellygrams had always been handled by three female students who majored in dance and enjoyed this ancient Middle Eastern art form.

"Well, we *guarantee* to please." Roxanne knew she had better. This was neither the time, place, nor people to fail. The Hepworth National Bank held her small-business loan, and Abraham Tyler would be the man to review its extension in three months.

The rear alcove of the office had been turned into a giant closet cum dressing area that held a wide range of costumes and a professionally lit makeup table. "First, a little mood music." Roxanne popped a cassette labeled *Raks Al-Sultan, Dance of the Sultans,* into the four-band portable stereo radio and cassette player before turning to the doorless wardrobe units.

A bass guitar and finger cymbals heralded an even rhythm in 4/4 time. The kanoon and oud, both string instruments, combined with drums, violin, and the wooden claves to add depth, while the alternately feminine high and masculine low tones of the oboe provided a decidedly sexual connotation.

Nothing in the room had been physically touched. Yet the atmosphere had changed, courtesy of the music. Gone was the warm but neuter work environment. In its place was an earthy aura of mystery, intrigue, and sensuality.

Roxanne tried to recall some of the finer points of the dance movements she had learned the week her jazzercise instructor had spent teaching the class belly dancing. She discovered it wasn't too difficult. The music seemed to demand an accompaniment of sinuous undulating movements that were at once graceful, supple, and fluid.

With little hesitation her right knee bent. Her left knee remained straight while her hips swayed from side to side in a horizontal figure eight to the provocative beat of the music. As the drum solo increased in intensity, Roxanne's hips crested into a shimmy-shake. The tempo slowed and she tried a belly roll, her lithe abdominal muscles rippling with sensual abandon beneath the punctilious business suit.

Visions of camels plodding through white desert sand toward a verdant oasis and a billowing tent drifted and formed in Roxanne's imagination. Her

hand paused on the shoulder of the gorilla costume, seeing not the grinning animal headpiece but a ruggedly handsome sheikh surrounded by the eager, enticing maidens of his harem.

"How silly!" she muttered, shaking her head sharply to disband those images and quickly zipped open the garment bag marked *Belly Dancer*. Roxanne began to effect her transformation.

The conservative double-breasted suit jacket was discarded along with a white long-sleeve blouse and bra. Roxanne frowned at the sequin- and coin-studded halter tops. The spangled bodice came only in small and medium sizes and both were modest garments on the lesser-developed college coeds. The medium, she ruefully discovered, provided only adequate covering for her full breasts. Roxanne eagerly hooked on a coin necklace that helped shelter her exposed cleavage.

Her gray flannel slim skirt, slip, and panty hose were the next to be shed. The costume's sapphire-blue silk skirt hung in panels from a wide belt of sequins, coins, and tassels that hugged her slim waist but dipped low enough in front to expose her belly button. Seven other scarves, in rainbow shades of blue, flowed down from the spangled girdle and swirled with each step around her long legs. Sequined coin anklets were clasped around each ankle and golden thongs extended between pale-pink toenails. A snake bracelet was slid on her upper arm.

With a small jeweled headpiece in hand, Roxanne moved toward the spotlight-rimmed mirror. "Well, the body doesn't look bad but the hair and face

19

. . ." She wiggled her nose at her reflection. Her light brown hair and rounded facial contours were a poor substitution for Leah Chang's raven waist-length silken mane and sloe-eyed Eurasian beauty.

Roxanne's brush fluffed through blond-highlighted shag-cut layers that bared her earlobes yet teased her nape. Her fingers reshaped the tousled curls that edged her forehead and cheeks. Hairpins anchored the sequined snood in place and the tiny blue silk veil that was attached left only wide brown eyes visible.

Dipping into the various cosmetic pots that littered the dressing table, Roxanne shadowed her eyelids in peach and teal, rimmed them with navy kohl liner, and applied two healthy coats of black mascara. Her tongue clicked against the roof of her mouth. "Bless you, Elizabeth Arden." A sultry eye lowered in a slow wink.

"Let's see . . ." Roxanne rubbed her hands together as she checked the appropriate list taped to the mirror. "One jewel for the belly button." A paste sapphire was installed courtesy of eyelash adhesive in her navel.

"Name and message decals." Humming along with the music, she rummaged in the drawer for a sheet of harmless transfers. The peel-off Arabic letters formed the word *Congratulations* across Roxanne's stomach and the swell of each breast was christened *Abe* and *Tyler*. A healthy cloud of Shalimar perfume completed her attire.

Roxanne's arms flowed like graceful snakes to the rhythm while belly and hips created beautiful feminine waves in the looking glass. The erotic reflection

in the mirror mesmerized and subtly elevated Roxanne's normally reserved sensibilities. The Middle Eastern music was decidedly wanton, the costume looked more provocative than ill-fitting, and belly dancing itself was proving to be a very sensual introduction to one's body.

She stared hard at her silk and jewel-ornamented anatomy. This was the exact same body Roxanne had inhabited for thirty years, and yet it looked different and felt foreign. A body that gifted visual pleasures and seemed quite capable of bestowing and receiving physical pleasures as well.

"How ridiculous!" Her harsh, self-chastising tone punctured the opiate illusion that had drugged her senses. "You are the same person whether wearing a business suit or this bit of fluff! Since when have you ever succumbed to such frivolous fantasies?"

Her shoulders wiggled uncomfortably, her fingertips absently scratching her bare midriff beneath the hanging chains and coins. "Actually this is downright itchy!" Her brief moment of admiration and self-passion was quick to reverse itself. "And more than a little degrading!" she snorted in disgust at the tattoos that adorned her anatomy. "Forgive me, Gloria Steinem, but I'm out to do a job. Nothing more!" She made a mental note to check with the three women who usually delivered the belly-grams, and if any of them wanted out of future assignments, they'd find their boss in total support.

Right this minute Roxanne had no choice; there were no substitutes available. Her straight nose wrinkled the silken veil. Funny, she mused, four years ago

21

she wouldn't have hesitated even a second about jumping into this costume to belly-dance a greeting. Occupying an executive position had changed her self-image and tempered her adventurous nature. Had she become rather stuffy and proper and maybe a bit too priggish and prim?

She laughed out loud at her reflection. Today would cure that. She savored the breezy lightness of the harem outfit in contrast to her heavy winter garb and felt buoyant and carefree. Where was it written that female executives couldn't be a little outrageous, a little avant garde, and totally lacking in decorum? "Gloria Steinem," came Roxanne's laughing addendum, "eat your heart out!"

Coined feet jingled their way into knee-high golden brown leather boots before Roxanne slipped her arms into a midcalf fur coat, shivering slightly as the cool amber silk lining came in contact with her bare skin. Her brown felt fedora was carefully placed over the costume's headpiece, the face veil stowed in her purse until later.

She had fifteen minutes to get to the Hepworth National Bank, which was located nine blocks across town by the Grain Exchange. Getting a taxi during the rush hour would be a time-wasting proposition, so she'd take the skyway system to her destination then walk the three blocks to pick up her car at the service garage where it was getting a new muffler and front brakes.

The stereo cassette player clasped in a gloved hand, Roxanne's last official act of the day and the year was to switch on the telephone-answering machine and lock the office door behind her.

Five minutes later the answering machine played a tuneful, musical message for the incoming caller. When the tone sounded, a deep chuckle recorded on the tape. "Hey, I like that, Miss Murdoch. This is Jerry at the garage. I hope you're on your way to get your car. We're closing early tonight because the storm is getting worse and we won't open again till next year!"

Once outside her office building on La Salle Court, Roxanne found herself caught in an eddy of stinging snow and quickly ran for the protection offered by the weatherproof skyway system. The network of second-level walkways interconnected throughout the heart of the city and on occasions like this provided a haven to residents from the near-Siberian cold.

Like most Minnesotans, Roxanne took winter in stride, but she had to admit this had been a particularly nasty year. "Worst storm of the century," had been the weather forecaster's cry three times so far, and it appeared Mother Nature had yet to exhaust herself!

Only an hour after sunset and the soft gray sky was heavily embittered with black-bottomed clouds. Roxanne found her usual blasé winter attitude altering rapidly. When she had left for work this morning the snowflakes had been big and feathery, like icy butterflies hovering over the landscape. Sometime during the day all that had changed. The snow had turned serious and anxious and wild. Despite the comfortable interior, hearing the steady pelting against the skyway's glass panes she turned up the wide collar on her coat.

Above her were the Plexiglas skylights that roofed the IDS Crystal Court. The fifty-seven-story Investors Diversified Building was bejeweled by blinking Christmas-tree lights, mechanical displays, and glitter, but sadly lacking in its usual human density. It also hadn't escaped Roxanne's attention that she was sharing the walkway with an ever-thinning, rapidly moving crowd. Swallowing hard, she increased her stride to a running gait and silently cursed her own stupidity for not listening to the weather or news reports during the day.

All too soon Roxanne had to leave the skyway system and take to the snow-covered, slippery sidewalks. Pulling the fedora's brim low and tight, and burying her face in the upraised fur collar, she plodded through the snow-filled alleys, letting the tall glass-and-concrete building shield her from the growing intensity of the storm.

Her gloved hand clasped the Hepworth Bank's huge circular outside doorknob just as the security guard's fingers closed around the interior handle. The man smiled, shook his head, and turned his digital watch toward her. Roxanne smiled back, fumbled in her coat pocket a second, then held her business card up to the glass. The door was promptly opened.

"Just about given you up for lost," his deep voice rumbled in greeting. "Bank's been like a tomb for the last hour." Keen blue eyes looked over her shoulder at the weather. "Rough as it looks?"

"Worse," came her breathless reply. "Traffic is either at a standstill or nonexistent." Roxanne greedily inhaled lungfuls of comforting warm air. "Where do I go?"

"Right through the main lobby to the red-doored elevator and up to the fourth floor. I'll buzz Mr. Carlin that you're on your way up." The gray-uniformed guard reached for the receiver of the phone intercom that hung on the wall.

Tomb was the appropriate word, Roxanne thought wryly, her eyes flicking over the harsh marble walls and heavily grilled teller cages. Even the twenty-foot gaily decorated Christmas tree did little to help soften the effect. She had to compress her lips to stifle the urge to liven the emptiness with a scream. Instead, Roxanne hit her boot's stacked heels a bit more forcefully against the beige and brown marble floor tiles, taking almost perverse satisfaction in the echoing ring that punctured the mausoleumlike quiet.

If Roxanne didn't know better, she'd swear the Hepworth National Bank was older than dirt. She had visions of the templelike structure standing proudly among the Sioux Indians' dome-shaped wigwams and one of its illustrious representatives scolding Father Louis Hennepin when he arrived in 1680 for leaving Belgium without traveler's checks.

To say the building itself was intimidating was an understatement, at least in Roxanne's viewpoint. The exterior boasted a Tuscan colonnade while the interior monochromatic decor did little to make anyone feel welcome. The entire effect translated into a pompous, cold, and somewhat threatening atmosphere that was tempered with a feeling of security, the wisdom of the ancients, and the knowledge that its investments were entrusted to omnipotent forces. And so, Roxanne, like the majority of the other two million Minneapolis residents, had made the Hepworth National Bank her bank.

The elevator responded immediately to her summons and whisked her with silent efficiency to the fourth floor. An expectant masculine face greeted her. "Mr. Carlin?" She extended a gloved hand.

"At last you're here." Bifocaled blue eyes blinked rapidly in relief. "We were afraid all our best-laid plans would go asunder."

"Greetings and Salutations guarantees delivery and satisfaction." Roxanne smiled an apology. "Where can I hang my coat and make a brief costume adjustment?"

"The employee's lounge is right here, or if you prefer the ladies' room?" Mr. Carlin inquired, his short, rotund figure pausing by a closed door.

"This will do nicely," Roxanne assured him.

"I'll get everyone into their proper positions and be right back for you. Mr. Tyler is under the impression this is just a combination New Year's and bon voyage office party we're throwing for him." A rather feminine burst of giggles slipped from Mr. Carlin's throat. "You'll really be a heart-stopper!"

"I hope old Abe Tyler has his digitalis handy," Roxanne mumbled, watching the banker's blue-business-suited figure waddle down the hallway and disappear around the corner.

The employees' lounge surprised her. The attractively decorated room contained all the warmth missing from the main lobby of the century-old building. Here hanging plants had been decorated with twinkling Christmas lights and tiny ornaments, candled centerpieces adorned the three dining tables, the window had been stain-glassed by a creative hand, and even the four massive vending machines were wreathed in a red and green garland.

Her eyes inspected the vending machines with sudden longing. How wonderful a hot cup of coffee or cocoa would taste right now. A gnawing in her stomach made her realize just how feeble a lunch she had consumed. Half a peanut butter and banana sandwich wasn't much to keep her five-foot-eight-inch one-hundred-thirty-five-pound body going for very long.

One machine held hamburgers, hot dogs, mini-pizzas, and burritos, all easily and quickly heated in the microwave on the kitchen counter. "Later," she promised, her finger tapping the glass in front of a beef and cheese enchilada. A little fuel for the three-block walk through the storm to retrieve her car couldn't hurt.

Roxanne fitted her remodeled fur coat around a wooden hanger, wrinkling her nose at the musty odor the dyed-to-look-like-red-fox raccoon pelts were emitting. The fedora came next, and using a wall-mounted mirror, she hastily brushed her hair, reattached the face veil, and straightened her costume. Her boots and purse were left beneath the coat on the lower rack of the office valet.

She decided to thread one of the silk scarves through the halter top, thereby covering the decals. "No sense giving poor old Abe too much of a shock all at once," Roxanne murmured with a grin.

Mr. Carlin opened the door just as Roxanne finished checking the stereo cassette machine. "Ready?" His facial expression was an appreciative tribute to her highly visual feminine charms.

"Ready," she echoed, falling into jingling steps beside him. "How will I know Mr. Tyler?"

"The secretary's pinned a mistletoe boutonniere on his suit jacket," Mr. Carlin informed her, his voice low and cautious.

Loud laughter and chatter, both male and female, greeted Roxanne as she made the hallway turn. Her hand caught the banker's coat sleeve. "If you'd just press this button to start the music," she whispered, and handed him the player unit.

Behind the partially open door an officious male voice boomed. "We have a little surprise for you. Something to make your Caribbean vacation a bit more memorable and a reason to make you more anxious to come back to the bank."

Mr. Carlin's pudgy thumb pressed the black start button. The kanoon, oud, and cymbals started the overture to the *Dance of the Sultans,* and Roxanne, her hands crossed demurely over her breasts, her eyes lowered in the proper subservient manner, entered the room and murmured, "Salaam."

CHAPTER TWO

Dark blue eyes widened with surprise and piqued masculine interest. "Well, J.D., is this your subtle way of telling me I'm going to a Middle Eastern branch and she'll be my secretary?"

"No, no." J. D. Wingate's blustery chuckle dwarfed the group's congenial laughter. "This is our subtle way of telling you that effective today you are now Senior Vice President Abraham Tyler. Congratulations!" The bank president's massive hand reached out to heartily grip his newly promoted officer's.

"This little lady," Mr. Carlin's jovial voice chimed, "comes to you courtesy of the rest of us senior vice presidents. She'll show you in veils just how high up the ladder you've been promoted," he added with a broad wink.

Roxanne's gaze was still focused on her feet as she half-listened to the chattering milieu while waiting for the percussion bridge to segue into the main musical movement. She felt inordinately pleased with herself. All the initial trepidation and discomfort she'd previous experienced had vanished. It seemed like old times! Right this minute she felt relaxed, confident, and deliciously heady. When the cymbals, wooden claves, and string instruments resumed their slow, introductory tempo, Roxanne became totally absorbed in delivering a winning performance.

Her right foot danced three steps to the measure. Each time her bare sole made full contact with the plush brown carpet the coins jingled with the rhythm. Head still lowered, Roxanne began to move her arms. Her hands bent at the wrists and rotated in complete circles to the exact timing of the music. Arms bent at the elbows made graceful, sinuous moves in all directions: over her head, down at her sides, one over her head and one down in front of her navel.

She lowered her arms to a horizontal position out at her side, then proceeded to raise one up and one down at the same time in a sensual rippling manner. As the high tones of the oboe drifted from the cassette, Roxanne slowly raised her head and moved it from side to side, using only her neck muscles, first to the right and then to the left.

Sultry, shadowed eyelids rose so Roxanne could view the effect all this was having on old Abraham Tyler. The darkened fringe of lashes fluttered in startled confusion as she blinked the object of her greeting into sharper focus. She had been expecting a replica of Abraham Lincoln replete with stovepipe hat and a log cabin tietack. But the man standing in front of her, the man wearing a mistletoe boutonniere and an engaging grin, was certainly no older than his mid-thirties.

Her mind registered a tall, lean but broad-shouldered physique that was defined to best advantage by an expertly tailored three-piece navy suit. His black hair shone with blue highlights distinguished by silver strands that accented strong features that were handsome in a not too overwhelming way.

The music increased in its urgency, forcing Roxanne back into more elaborate motion. She had no time to further contemplate the Hepworth National Bank's new seventh senior vice president. *Indeed,* she mused, bringing her hips forward as her abdominal muscles pushed in and out in an undulating belly roll, *I'd better not think about Abraham Tyler at all. This is just a sliver in time; he is just the recipient of a greeting. Do the best job possible then exit rapidly.*

Comfortably ensconced on the corner of his free-form walnut desk, Bram Tyler took leisurely inventory of the delightful feminine silhouette sensuously twisting and turning in sequined and gold splendor just for him. A smile lifted the corners of his mouth. The dancer was certainly one of his dream fantasies come true. Now, if only the room didn't contain such a crowd!

A series of jingling, intricate foot movements lured his attention to her feet. His gaze traveled from their sexy bareness up long shapely calves and sleek thighs that disappeared into a slither of rounded hip beneath the coin-and-chain girdle. Bram was watching her swaying hips move from side to side in a horizontal figure eight when a pale blue scarf fluttered toward him and clung provocatively to his jacket.

Her hips matched the fervor of the music. The gossamer silk skirt appeared weightless. Bram followed the swirling sapphire around her legs and watched it fill the air with magic color. The intoxicating scent of her perfume beckoned to him every time she moved and he found the fragrance enormously appealing. Two more scarves waved fingerlike toward Bram. Now there was just enough silk left to make him wonder what she would look like in less and less.

The oboe's serpentine tones were interpreted in the waving motions that rippled the word *Congratulations* on her belly. She turned around and Bram's eyes traveled the supple length of her spine and her smoothly tapered back. Her shoulders, arms, hands, hips, and belly moved with fluid, well-toned grace. He collected yet another azure scarf, the essence of jasmine and roses increased vividly in his arms.

But the diaphanous squares of silk were a poor substitute for embracing the real woman. And Bram discovered he had to temper an overwhelming urge to do just that. While he couldn't touch, he could look, and his eyes celebrated the subtle sexiness of the veiled dancer.

Subtle, yes, that was the perfect word, came his silent pronouncement. Bram couldn't deny the wanton music, the undulating body, and the perfumed scarves were having a devastating effect on his anatomy. Yet despite the costume and the sensual dance, the woman didn't appear to have any hard edges.

There was something about the belly dancer that was more wholesome than exotic. She seemed totally unconscious of her allure, rather than a practiced courtesan, well-versed in female games. Maybe it was the hesitant steps in her recital or the soft lightness of her curly hair or . . . Amid his colleagues' applause and whistles, Bram reached out, securing two more lengths of silk.

Preoccupied and intrigued with the woman rather than the dance, Bram focused on her face, and for the first time noticed the pink blush that glowed above the blue veil. Her eyes became impossible not to stare at. Brown irises rimmed in smoky darkness—two potent communicators that looked at once seductive and innocent but still had the ability to make his toes tingle and curl inside his black leather shoes. She looked so soft and feminine that it made him feel more masculine and stronger than he was.

The *Dance of the Sultans* was raging toward a crescendo. Bram watched her shoulders quiver to the feverish tempo. As she bent backward, long, slender fingers slowly pulled a scarf through the top of her sequined halter, exposing more and more velvety cleavage. His ever-widening eyes discovered that the full swells of her breasts bore his name.

Bram tried to remain sober and keep his wits about him despite the fact he seemed to be suffering from localized muscle pressure, an increased pulse rate, and sweaty palms. The rhythm grew frenzied and urgent. Mesmerized, he stared as she whirled like a zealous dervish, hips increasing into a shimmy, and then suddenly everything exploded in silence. She looped the final scarf around his neck, one shadowed eye lowered in a wink, and Bram watched as she quickly turned and sprinted out the door amid thunderous applause.

Roxanne didn't stop running until she literally fell through the door of the employees' lounge and collapsed in a breathless heap on the tweed pillow-back love seat. Her heart had jumped from her breast to pound out of control in her throat. No wonder belly dancing was listed as more exercise than dance, came Roxanne's dizzy appraisal; in the last ten minutes she had used and exhausted more muscles than she'd ever known she possessed!

Yanking the veil from her face in an effort to catch a full breath, Roxanne put her fingertips to her diaphragm and tried to control her erratic panting. She inhaled slowly and deeply and after three good breaths felt much calmer and less tense. But all that changed the instant the door swung open. Her eyes and stomach both clenched at the thought of the intruder being Abraham Tyler, but she relaxed when she heard Mr. Carlin's high-pitched voice.

"You were wonderful. Simply marvelous." The portly banker waddled over to the sofa, leaving the cassette recorder on the end table. "You know, my sixtieth birthday is next month." A beefy hand smoothed the thin layer of brown hair that barely shielded his balding pate. "Would it be possible for you to . . ."

Assuming a more professional posture, Roxanne gave him an equally proficient smile. "Certainly, just give Greetings and Salutations a call, telling us the date, time, and location, and we'll be delighted to issue you a belly-gram."

"I will. I will." His ruddy face bobbed eagerly in the loose collar of his white shirt. "I was hoping . . . I mean, we all were . . ." He fiddled with the buttons on his vest, his eyes trying not to stare at her voluptuous bodice. "Would you care to join in on the last few minutes of our celebration? They're serving champagne," he added hopefully.

"Thank you, but that's against company policy." She softened her refusal with another smile. "I'm just going to relax here for a minute and then leave. Do I take the same red elevator down to the bank?"

"No, that one's locked," Mr. Carlin informed her. "Continue to walk around the corner and take the black one. It opens on the covered parking area and drive-in teller windows." With a reluctant sigh he said a final good-bye and left.

Roxanne quickly rose and locked the door, making certain no one else would walk in on her. She surveyed her skimpy outfit, wrinkled a rueful nose, and wished she had thought of bringing along her suit. Her fingertips were idly scratching the itchiness caused by the chains and sequins that irritated her sensitive skin when her stomach made a low, grumbling sound.

"I did promise you food, didn't I?" She grinned and looked at the wall clock. It was only six thirty, and since the service garage didn't close until eight Roxanne had plenty of time to recoup her energy and fortify herself with the promised coffee and burrito.

She took a handful of loose change from the pocket of her coat, tumbled the appropriate coins in the vending machine slot, and pressed the buttons for her selection. The enticing aroma of coffee filled the room while Roxanne read and followed the microwave instructions on the plastic wrapper of the ice-cold burrito. Four minutes later she was energetically waving curls of steam from the hot items so they could be savored and enjoyed.

Three more trips to the vending machine bought her another cup filled with surprisingly good coffee, a packet of tortilla chips, and a fudge brownie. With her legs stretched out on a second dining chair, Roxanne leisurely perused the morning newspaper and then found herself absorbed in an article on successful entrepreneurs in a trade banker's magazine.

As the last morsel of brownie was lifted to her mouth, only then did Roxanne notice the time. "Seven fifteen!" She became a rapidly moving mass of arms and legs. Garbage was dumped into the trash can, crumbs swept off the table followed suit, and the two chairs were put in their proper places.

Roxanne dressed with the precise haste of a fireman. With her purse thrown over her shoulder and the lightweight cassette player gripped in a gloved hand, she snapped off the lights, opened the door, and stepped into the hallway.

The silence was deafening. Only every third ceiling light was on, giving Roxanne the uncomfortable feeling she was the sole living occupant of the building. *How stupid to sit for so long,* she silently berated herself. *It would serve you right to be trapped here till tomorrow!* A silly grin spread over her lips. *I wonder what the penalty is for running barefoot through all the money in the vault?*

Her boots moved soundlessly along the carpeted hallway, and as she angled around the corner she spotted the red exit sign over the black-doored elevator. When the doors opened Roxanne exhaled a pent-up breath of relief. "Almost home free."

"Hold that door, please!" A deep masculine voice sliced the quiet.

Her hand hit the appropriate button at the same time she looked over her shoulder at the tall figure coming down the opposite corridor. Brown eyes squinted to concentrate the subdued lighting, then widened in horrified recognition. "Oh, no!" she bubbled. Why him? Why Abraham Tyler? Why not the more easily handled Mr. Carlin?

Pulling the brim of her fedora low on her forehead, Roxanne stepped as deep into the elevator's far corner as was humanly possible. She wasn't quite sure why she had concluded that Abraham Tyler couldn't be easily handled. Perhaps it was a subconscious act based on a first impression. She remembered the expression on his face and the gleam in his blue eyes while he assessed her dancing. Abraham Tyler might have been smiling, but that hadn't negated the resilience in his features.

"Thanks for waiting." Bram nodded, a blunt forefinger pressed the down button, and the doors slid closed. "Didn't realize anyone else was still here."

A noncommittal "Hmmmm" was issued by Roxanne while she tried to shield the cassette machine in the full folds of her coat.

"All set for a big New Year's Eve?"

"Huh, huh." She grimaced at her neanderthal response. Damn the man! Didn't he know that silence was the only proper etiquette for elevators? Damn this elevator! Did it have to creak downward at such a snail's pace?

"Well, tomorrow morning I'll be basking in the warm Caribbean sunshine, playing some tennis, doing some scuba diving, trying my luck in the casinos." When he received yet another monosyllabic reply, Bram lowered his head, trying for a better view of the face under the hat. The brim shielded all but the tip of the woman's nose, a rounded curve of her left cheek, a gold-studded earlobe glimpsed through a wispy tendril of brown-blond hair, a softly delineated jawline, and even, white teeth gnawing at a full bottom lip.

Roxanne's mouth felt filled with cotton; her palms soaked the lining of her leather gloves. She tilted her head sideways and lowered her chin. For every inch Abraham Tyler lowered his head in an effort to see her Roxanne lowered hers even farther until her chin bumped into a fur lapel.

Bram raised his head, his fingers ruffling the short sideburn by his right ear. "Weren't you one of the secretaries at my party?"

"Noooo." The odd high-pitched answer wasn't exactly a lie, Roxanne told herself; she wasn't a secretary. She caught his head making a quick downward motion and again managed to twist her face out of

38

sight. The toe of her boot tapped an impatient tattoo against the elevator floor. What was taking this archaic vehicle so long!

Roxanne began to feel quite sick to her stomach and itchy all over. When she heard the rumble of his voice begin to ask another question, her abdomen clenched inward in a sharp muscle spasm. Beneath the safety of her coat, she relaxed her stomach, pushing out, hoping the expansion would eliminate the pain.

A tiny *ping* assaulted her ears. Her eyes lowered, her breath strangled in her throat as the dime-sized fake sapphire from her belly button bounced from the floor, off the top of her boot, to land between her left foot and his right. As unobtrusively as possible, Roxanne edged the vamp of her boot toward the glossy blue stone.

An inch from concealing her lost treasure, a large male hand circumvented her efforts by trapping her ankle. "Tut, tut. Don't deny me another charming souvenir." His resonant voice brimmed with laughter. "This gem will go so well with my new scarf collection."

Her shoulders hunched, Roxanne's expression soured at the attractive masculine face grinning up at her. Normally some clever, witty retort would have zinged from her lips, but like a rabbit hypnotized by a snake, she had stared at Abraham Tyler a fraction of a second too long to render any brilliant quip.

Her only reaction was silence. A silence wrought with sudden vulnerability. An inner battle raged, and

Roxanne fought to become the victor. She threw back her shoulders and tried to muster some shred of haughty dignity. She was an executive, for heaven's sake—her company's president. She should be able to come back with something appropriately glib and profound. But her only reply was to lift the coat's wide collar and pray that Abraham Tyler would dispense with further comments on her scanty attire, or her dancing.

The elevator doors mercifully clanked open. Eyes and features completely devoid of expression, Roxanne made a rude, rapid exit. Her long strides took her from the safe concrete roof of the banking and parking shelter into a snowy, wind-whipped frenzy.

Roxanne stood stupefied in a knee-high drift for a moment. She had thought the random squall would have disappeared. Instead, the weather seemed to be enjoying a full head of blizzard havoc. Shielding her face from the stinging maelstrom as best she could with her hat and her upturned collar, Roxanne plodded through the snowy architecture that blanketed the sidewalks. It was going to be a long three blocks to Jerry's garage.

Ice had formed beneath the heavy, wet snow, making normal walking impossible. Roxanne maneuvered with marginal success by skating and shuffling along the perilous pavement. Her feet were rapidly feeling the low temperature despite the fur lining in her boots.

A car horn bleated through the howling din, its head- and foglights casting her in an amber glow. "Did you break down?"

Roxanne slid toward the stopped brown sedan and the yelling male voice. "No. My car's garaged around the corner at Washington," she yelled to the unseen occupant through the two-inch opening on the side window.

"Get in and I'll give you a lift. I drive right by there."

She hesitated but then her gloved hand waved him on. "No thanks, I'll be fine."

The window finished rolling down. "Get in, lady of the seven veils, before your belly freezes!"

A groan escaped Roxanne. "Couldn't you have turned in the other direction, Abraham Tyler?" she groused loudly.

"It's a one-way street," Bram reminded her with a grin. "Come on, I'm not taking no for an answer."

Roxanne didn't try to stifle a sigh of relief as she slid into the Mercury Zephyr's warm interior. "I was sure the storm would have worn itself out by now," she breathed, cradling the cassette player and her purse between her knees. Then, taking a deep breath, she added, "Thank you for the lift."

"My pleasure. I feel very possessive and protective about a woman who has my name tattooed on her—"

"Mr. Tyler," Roxanne's warning tone quickly interrupted his statement. "I should think a banker would have more respect for those who are gainfully employed. If you're going to continue to levy these insults, I can easily walk to my car." She turned more fully toward him, her angry expression visible under the dome light. "I'm from Chicago and to me

41

this"—her hand gestured toward the outdoors—"is just a stiff breeze."

Bram merely stared at her, his blue eyes locking into her snapping brown ones, his ears enjoying the husky timbre of her angry tirade. His subconscious whispered a feeling of déjà vu. He knew this woman; now, if he could just coordinate the face, the voice, and a name. Suddenly Bram snapped his fingers. "You're the graph lady!"

Roxanne went from pale to pink at again hearing that phrase. "It . . . it can't be you." Her tongue moistened her dry lips. "The loan officer I dealt with had a . . . a beard and moustache and—"

"That was me," he said with a grin and an inner feeling of satisfaction at her remembering. "You caught me the first day back from a fishing vacation in the mountains." Bram notched the stick shift from park to drive, frowning as the rear tires spun a few times before finding traction. "Roxanne Murdoch, president of Greetings and Salutations."

She listened in amazement while he recited her home address and even her phone number. "I had no idea you possessed a photographic memory."

"Only when it's important to me," came his easy rejoinder. "I was impressed with your business acumen. You came prepared with everything from color graphs to flow charts. You answered my five major investment questions in ninety seconds, had a stunning business summary, and appeared calm and personable but professional. As a matter of fact, I was highly impressed with you personally." His gaze briefly left the windshield to glance at her. "I even

42

liked the black and white dress and red jacket you wore."

Roxanne inhaled sharply, her gloved fingers digging into the beige velveteen bucket seat. Even she couldn't recall what she'd worn! "Thank you." Those were the only two coherent words she could manage.

Bram's pensive expression had little to do with road conditions. "Are you having some business problems?" he asked. "I know your loan was meant to expand your greeting company, move into a downtown office, and hire personnel. We do have a staff of specially trained advisors that are available to help small businesses."

"Why is it you're so quick to assume that my business is in trouble?" Roxanne rushed in defensively. "I have never been late, let alone missed a loan payment. You have my house and my car as collateral, I'm paying nearly three points over the prime rate for interest, you're processing my payroll, and just because I'm a woman, you—"

"Did you know that nearly three million women own their own small firms?" Bram interjected in a soothing tone. "As a matter of fact, twenty-five percent of all small businesses in the United States are owned by women. I think women are a great investment, hence the reason I approved your loan in less than an hour, Roxanne Murdoch."

"I was just curious as to why *you* happened to be on the delivery end today?" His hands tightened at the nine o'clock and three o'clock positions on the steering wheel to better control the car's slow progress. The rapidly accumulating snow and heavy winds had just about obliterated the previous tire tracks on the road. Bram was supremely conscious of the fact that his rearview mirror hadn't reflected any headlights since he had left the bank's parking lot.

"Because my regular dancer fell and broke her ankle on the way to work and no one else was available," Roxanne explained after digesting his previous statements. "You lost out," she added dryly. "Leah is not only an expert belly dancer but a very exotic, beautiful one at that."

"Oh, I don't know. I'd say my loss was also my gain."

She decided to ignore his comment. "Business is booming, by the way," came her swift retort.

Bram laughed and nodded appreciatively. "I believe you." He switched the windshield wipers from medium to high and increased the strength of the defroster, but visibility was getting poorer. "That pertinacious personality of yours is what inhibited my first instincts toward you."

Roxanne turned her head. "I beg your pardon?"

"I had every intention of inviting you out for dinner after we'd finished filling out all the forms. But you were so much on the defensive, so well prepared with your graphs and charts and statements and outlines to give me a hell of a fight over the loan that I just knew you'd refuse out of principle. Probably think I had an ulterior motive."

"There you go jumping to conclusions again," she

pounced back. "Now you think you know what goes on in my mind!"

The left side of his mouth quirked. "You mean you would have gone out with me?"

"Absolutely," she said with righteous indignation.

"How about two weeks from tomorrow, when I return from my vacation?"

"Fine with me," Roxanne enunciated each word forcefully.

"Dinner and the theater?"

"Wonderful."

Bram coughed to cover a laugh. Her acceptance sounded more like a threat. He felt in his legs he had turned the corner too fast, the rear wheels sliding to the left before straightening. "I hope the weather at thirty-five thousand feet is better than this."

"You don't seriously think your plane is going to take off tonight, do you?" Roxanne asked in amazement.

"Well, the radio didn't report the airport closed twenty minutes ago and my plane doesn't leave till ten. This could all be over by then."

"You're very optimistic, Abraham Tyler. Oh, Jerry's garage is on this corner." She tapped the side window, gesturing toward the building's glowing red neon sign. "Right here."

He eased his foot off the accelerator and pumped the brakes gently, the sedan fishtailing to a halt. "By the way, no one has called me Abraham or Abe since the nurse in the hospital filled out my birth certificate. It's Bram." He reached up to switch on the dome light. "Are you always called Roxanne?"

45

Her smile was shielded as she picked up her purse and recorder. "My brothers call me Rocky and my parents always say Roxy."

"Then just to keep in the mood with your fantasy image, I'll stick with Roxanne." Bram's voice was low and compelling. "After all, to Cyrano de Bergerac, the fabled Roxane was the ideal of womanhood, the symbol of beauty that all men desire." He tugged the brim of her fedora.

The wicked glint in Roxanne's brown eyes surpassed that of Bram's blue ones. Her gloved index finger reached to stroke the length of his nose; her tone was saccharine sweet. "Isn't it a shame you don't possess Cyrano's legendary nose—then we could both indulge in a fantasy!" She opened the door and swung her legs out. "Thanks again for the lift." His "see you in two weeks" was issued only a second before she slammed the passenger door.

The front door of Jerry's boasted a huge plastic Santa imprisoned behind a security grill and a warning sign about a burglar alarm. Roxanne trudged through the knee-high drifts toward the rear garage doors, keeping close to the massive building and using the wide overhang for protection against the wind.

Her breathing coming in jerky gasps, Roxanne pounded on the wire mesh windows, but no one answered her barrage. Putting her face tight against the icy glass, she could see her yellow Toyota snug and safe inside, but it had no human companions. "Great!" her leathered fist hit the door one more time. "Now what do I do?"

Roxanne realized trying to find any public transportation on a night like this was a gesture in futility. She took a realistic examination of the situation and decided to walk back the blocks necessary to catch the skyway system and return to her office. At least she'd spend the night in warm, safe surroundings.

Halfway around the garage, Roxanne stumbled into Bram. "What are you still doing here?"

CHAPTER THREE

"Making sure you're all right." Bram's hands curled around her upper arms to guide her more fully under the wide protective eaves. "Where's your car?" His fingers ruffled the snow from amber-toned pelts. "Isn't it ready?"

"Ready, waiting, and locked in," Roxanne made the glum announcement. "Better late than never is not one of those clever axioms that auto garages subscribe to."

"Come on, I'll drive you home. The eight o'clock news reported the airport has been shut down." Turning up the collar on his cashmere and wool topcoat, Bram bleakly surveyed the huge snowdrifts that resembled a wall of ocean breakers. "I guess I'll see one day less of St. Croix."

Further conversation became impossible due to the surging wind velocity that sent pellets of ice and snow stinging against them. When Roxanne finally tumbled into the front seat of the car, her first coherent sentence was a chastising one. "Where are your boots, gloves, and hat? I bet you don't even have a shovel or extra gasoline in the trunk."

"That's right, Mom." Bram shook his head toward her, sending a shower of snow in all directions. The dome light showed his boyish grin. "Do diehard residents of Minneapolis ever pay any attention to blizzard warnings? Snow is a way of life, so is the cold, you roll with Mother Nature's punches."

He buckled on his shoulder strap and safety belt before shifting the car into drive. The rear wheels made a furious grinding noise as the front end slid out of the parking lot into the main street.

"If they closed the airport," Roxanne mused, twisting toward him, "they must have closed the highways too. Maybe it would be smarter just to drop me at the skyway and I'll walk back to my office and spend the night there. Maybe you'd better stay at a hotel."

"Don't worry, the snow plows and sanding trucks are out there making Route 20 safe for humanity," he countered easily. "Besides, your house is right on my way home."

Roxanne's gloved hand wiped the interior condensation from her side window, but the view didn't improve. All that was visible was a churning mass of white. "You are the most optimistic optimist I've ever met." With a musical sigh, she settled into the bucket seat.

Bram wasn't quite sure when he started to whistle. It was about the same time his fingers became numb around the steering wheel as he waged a tiring battle to maintain control of the car. While whistling did seem to keep up the old courage, it didn't help with the driving. The combination of high winds and the icy snow-covered pavement sent the Zephyr sideways down Hennepin Avenue.

Front-wheel drive, rear-wheel drive, Bram doubted even having a four-wheel-drive vehicle would make any real difference. For once he should have listened to the travel advisories—it was insane to try to navigate out of doors tonight. Snowbound cars loomed like white giants in the amber glow of the sedan's fog lights and headlights. Negotiating around the abandoned autos took all his concentration.

Despite Bram's considerable driving skill, the Mercury went into an uncontrollable skid. He tried to make all the right moves and not panic. Lifting his foot off the gas, he turned the wheels into the skid. The car snapped back too fast and started skidding in the opposite direction. Bram fought with the steering wheel, whipping it around to straighten the course, but the sedan defied him at every turn.

Roxanne had been holding her breath since the third skid. Her eyes shifted back and forth from Bram's profile to the windshield. There was no use in denying their hazardous position. She wished she could do something, anything, but she was totally helpless, totally useless. There was no denying her fear, yet Roxanne felt every confidence in the man at the wheel.

The Mercury Zephyr had aimed itself like a missile toward the side of the public library. Bram knew the chances of surviving a head-on collision with anything were not good. He had no choice but to swerve to the right.

The car spun like a wild top. Bram found muscles in his hands and arms he never knew existed. He used their strength to try to regain control. The sedan slid, slipped, and hydroplaned down Marquette Avenue toward a mountain of snow that edged the Federal Court House parking lot. Bram directed the car at the drift, but the snow proved to be harboring a very solid enemy—a steel guard rail.

The sound of mangled steel echoed above the wind. On impact, Bram's chest hit the steering wheel. The safety-collapsing mechanism and his shoulder harness took the brunt of the force but the blow knocked all the air from his lungs, leaving him momentarily stunned and gasping for breath.

For one second Roxanne thought she had died. There was a roaring in her ears and brilliant stars flashed and exploded in front of her eyes. But the pain in her head, right shoulder, and elbow made her realize that she was still among the living. Sliding her head from where it had made a hard, rather rude encounter with the steel windshield post, Roxanne's cheek discovered the cold windowpane. Her eyelids drifted closed as she enjoyed the glass's icy comfort.

Her frigid serenity was abruptly invaded by two rough hands and a frantic loud voice that kept repeating her name. "Are you all right? Roxanne? My God, what have I done? Roxanne!"

Roxanne reached to rescue and correctly position her hat. "For heaven's sake, what is all the shouting about?" She shivered against the foreign warm liquid

51

that trickled down her right temple, around her ear and along her nape.

Bram snapped on the dome light and peered into her face. Vacant brown eyes stared back. "Do you know who I am?" he demanded.

"Of course, you're . . . hmmm." She discovered she had to think about that for a moment. "Honest Abe," came her rather offhanded but triumphant announcement.

"I'll take that," he sighed. "Do you know who you are? Do you know where you are? Oh, hell!" Bram interrupted himself when he saw billowing puffs of smoke surpassing the blizzard. "We've got to get out of here." His hands snapped her shoulders. "I think we're on fire."

"Fire? Hmmm, that sounds nice and cozy."

"Oh . . . damn." With a great deal of reluctance, he began to lightly slap her face. "Come on, Roxanne, snap out of it. Come on, get moving."

Her disorientation fled. "Hey!" Roxanne's arm moved to block his. "Didn't your mother ever tell you that's no way to treat a lady!"

"You're back!" Bram exhaled a pent-up breath.

"Did I go someplace?"

"Mentally, and now you're going physically." He pointed toward the heavy white coating of hoarfrost that was forming in sheets on the windshield. "I'm not sure whether the radiator's been punctured or all that smoke is from a ruptured fuel line. The bank's only half a block from here. Think you can make it?"

"Of course."

"Don't leave anything," Bram directed, reaching

in the backseat for the leather attaché case that had been his father's. "Let's go."

Grabbing her purse and the cassette recorder, Roxanne tried to open the passenger door but found it jammed shut. "Wait a minute, I'm right behind you." She scrambled across the front seat and slid out on the driver's side.

The tiny beam on his pen-sized flashlight was a trifling aid. Bram shoved it back into his pocket, took possession of her recorder, which he juggled with his briefcase in his right hand. "Come on, this way," he screamed above the snowy cyclone that surrounded them. Cupping her right elbow in his left hand, Bram led Roxanne away from the smoking wreck.

They moved south on Third Street. Icy gale-force winds attacked them on all sides. The knee-high snow camouflaged the perilous terrain that soon sent them sprawling.

Bram crawled over to Roxanne and put his mouth next to her ear. "Come on, we're almost there." Steadying each other, they resumed their crouched vertical positions and continued to make slow headway against the turbulent gusts.

Head down, face buried between her hat and coat collar, Roxanne put more vigilance and caution in every step. It wasn't difficult, but her legs ached from plowing through snowbanks. There seemed no end to the snow, no relief in sight. In fact, to Roxanne the snow was looking pretty attractive—like a fluffy white comforter.

No, no, that's not right! She regained her sanity and blinked away the mirage. Roxanne wasn't quite sure what kept her going. Perhaps it was an instinct for survival, perhaps it was the fear of knowing a popsicle's death, or perhaps it was the extra support from the masculine arm that was wrapped around her waist. Quite probably it was all those things plus the continual reciting of all the prayers she had ever learned in Sunday School.

Bram's "There it is!" roared above the wind. Roxanne's left eye came out of seclusion and tried to make sense of where she was. The streetlights and the snow had combined to white out the night. Whatever *it* was, to Roxanne *it* was invisible. Lifting her head, she stared harder and was finally able to discern a vague darkish shadow. *It* proved to be the Hepworth National Bank.

When he started to guide her away from it, she struggled and they both ended up on their knees in a waist-high drift. "There!" Roxanne pointed to the left.

"There." Bram corrected her, nodding a snow-covered head to the right. "Come on." He slid back onto his frozen feet and helped her up. The last dozen steps proved the coldest, the windiest, and the longest he had ever traveled.

The instant they stepped beneath the protective concrete overhead on the bank's drive-through teller station, the momentum of the blizzard ceased. "We can take the elevator upstairs." Bram shook some snow off and stamped his way to the elevator, leaving a snowy wake. He wiggled a blotchy red hand into his coat pocket. Tingling fingers pinched at the elusive key case and ultimately dropped it on the ground. He lifted his white-knuckled hand to his mouth and tried to warm it back into functional operation with his breath.

Roxanne wheezed as she bent to retrieve the keys. "Why don't we just pound for the guard?"

"No guards. All electronic. Money's safe behind the vault's time lock." He tried flexing his fingers, hoping to improve both color and coordination. "You'd better do it. First the round alarm key and then the one with the blue plastic cap."

When the black doors slid open, they used their last burst of adrenaline to collapse in exhausted heaps on the floor and simultaneously lifted their frozen faces toward the heat duct.

"Are you okay?"

"Hmmm."

Despite the pain, Bram's lips formed a smile. "Is that your standard elevator conversation?" He opened his eyes and looked at her.

"Hmmm. Hmmm." Roxanne struggled into a sitting position, her back supported by an oak-paneled wall. "How are your hands?"

He was still blowing on them. "Coming along. Gloves are number one on my shopping list."

"What about your feet?"

"My feet?" Blue eyes blinked questioningly.

"Mine are like ice and they're in fur-lined boots." She crawled on all fours until she reached his shoes. "Can you feel them?"

"They hurt." He watched Roxanne work off his snow-packed black leather loafers and peel down his socks.

"That's a good sign." She pulled off her gloves and began to briskly rub the tops and soles of his bare feet with her hands.

"What are you doing?"

"Getting the old blood circulating," Roxanne told him matter-of-factly. "You keep working on your hands, frostnip isn't anything to ignore. When this charming contraption finally makes it upstairs, you can soak your hands and feet in a sinkful of warm water."

"Damn it, Roxanne, stop that right now!" Bram's tone reflected his growing self-condemnation. He twisted his ankles free and repostured himself Indian-style. "I nearly kill you and you're concerned about my feet! I'm the one—"

"Kill me!" She tried to pry loose a half-hidden foot. "Why that's the craziest thing." Roxanne yanked off her fedora and swatted his knee with it. "You handled that car like a Grand Prix driver." Ignoring his sudden intake of breath, she fixed him with her most intimidating stare. "You didn't panic, you didn't freeze, I was never afraid and—"

Suddenly Roxanne found herself imprisoned by his arms, his cold, firm mouth covering hers and consuming her words. Then just as abruptly she was released. "What . . . what . . ." She swallowed hard and stared at him. "Why did you do that?"

"Mouth-to-mouth resuscitation," Bram growled.

"But . . . but I didn't lose my breath."

"I did." His hand went to her right temple. "When I saw the blood on your face."

"Blood?" Her hollow echo reflected her dazed look.

Gentle masculine fingers carefully examined the scalp above her right ear. "Not only is the skin broken, but you've got a lump the size of an egg and . . ." Blue eyes focused on her brown ones and noted one dilated pupil and one pinpointed. "A concussion."

"No?"

"Yes." Lifting her chin, Bram scrutinized her winter-flushed features. "Have you got a headache? Are you dizzy? Nauseated? How do you feel?"

"Cold, wet and"—her mouth dropped at the edges—"very mortal. I could really use a hug."

"My pleasure." Again his arms embraced her. "One more inch and you'd have been dead."

Roxanne felt him shudder and her own arms tightened around his neck. "I was never in any danger; you're too good a driver." Her fingers ruffled the wet coils of black hair on his nape. "At any rate, I should have been wearing my seat belt."

"How are you feeling, really?"

"I've got a little headache," she admitted, then was silent for a moment, enjoying the sinewy solace he was providing. "Your poor car."

Bram nuzzled his face closer into the curve of her neck. "Don't worry about the car; it belongs to the bank and it's leased."

"Ah-ha! So that's where my extra interest points go."

"I can see a concussion didn't damage the humor cells in your brain." His nose twitched. "Roxanne, I

57

hate to tell you this." Bram pulled back. "Your coat smells the way my German shepherd did when he had a run-in with a skunk. I didn't know fox—"

Her giggles interrupted him. "It's raccoon and older than I am. I had it dyed, glazed, and reshaped as a Christmas present to myself. The last time this coat saw any action was in a rumble seat on the way to dance the Charleston." Roxanne took a whiff of her sleeve and made a face. "Back to the furrier and more reconditioning."

The elevator doors creaked open. "Speaking of reconditioning, let's get to work on us," Bram ordered as he collected their scattered belongings. "There's a first aid kit in the lounge. I want to put some antiseptic on that cut."

Roxanne trailed after him down the corridor. "But Bram, I'm—"

"No buts." The overhead light snapped into obedient service. "Out of that coat," he directed her. After divesting himself of his own topcoat, he took her fur and hung them both on the valet. "You take off those boots while I get us some liquid warmth." Bram moved to the hot-drink machine, tumbled in some coins, and a minute later was the recipient of two steaming cups. "Chicken soup."

Roxanne eagerly accepted the broth. "Better than Mother's homemade," came her sighed pronouncement. She twisted in the dining chair to dangle chafed feet over the floor heating duct. Presently, two more feet came to enjoy the warmth. "I think I'm beginning to defrost," she told Bram between mouthfuls of soup.

"Let me get you patched up." He found the white and blue first aid kit in the cabinet over the sink. Bram took a minute to wash his hands and brought some wet paper towels back with him to the table. "The doctor is in." His carefree voice belied his inner concern. Now both Roxanne's pupils were dilated and Bram had a hunch that her head ached more than she was admitting.

On hearing his second "hmmm" Roxanne pulled the lapels on his jacket. "You're beginning to sound like me in the elevator."

Bram viewed her through a bridge of arms. "This does not look good. You should have X rays and stitches."

"Scalp wounds are notoriously ugly and look much worse than they are. Just smush the skin together and hold it with adhesive."

"Thank you, Florence Nightingale," came his wry quip as he tossed a second bloodstained paper towel in the direction of the wastebasket. "Where did you get your medical training?"

"I have four younger brothers who keep Band-Aid in business," she winced as he resumed working on her head wound.

"Four? How old are they?" Bram selected a tube of ointment and carefully read the instructions.

"Fifteen and thirteen."

"And the other two?"

"They're two sets of twins," Roxanne informed him. Her lips twisted into a frown at the yellowish-blue discoloration on her right elbow. She looked like she'd been in a war and lost!

59

"That's quite a family. Bend your head toward me just a bit more; this shouldn't hurt." Bram squeezed a white line of anti-bacterial ointment on her scalp. "I'm going to put on a gauze bandage to keep these curls from sticking." He ripped open a sterile packet, placed the pad on her head, and caught the ends with adhesive strips. As he checked the security of the dressing, Bram's mind finally comprehended what she had said. "Twin brothers fifteen and thirteen?"

Roxanne managed a smile despite her growing discomfort. "I was wondering which one of us had the concussion."

"That's an age gap of—"

"Fifteen years," she supplied. "That story is an instant conversation starter."

"I'll bet. How about another cup of soup and you can regale me with all the details?"

"No, thanks. I'm fine."

The lowness of Roxanne's usually full voice made Bram turn from the vending machine. "You're not fine, are you?"

She gave an offhanded shrug and swallowed down a persistent burning in her throat. "I'm just feeling as worn out as my poor old coat." Roxanne hastily decided to change the subject. "This poor costume!" She viewed the torn, water-stained skirt, the broken chains, and spaces where coins and sequins had adorned wide hip girdle and halter. "I don't think snow and silk are at all compatible."

"As much as I enjoy looking at you in that outfit" —Bram flashed a purely masculine smile—"why don't I see if I can find you something to change into.

60

On occasion a secretary will leave her dry cleaning or even an extra dress."

While Bram went to explore any unlocked offices and closets, Roxanne spread his navy socks over the heat duct and relocated his shoes closer to the warm air. But just those small exertions made her dizzy and brought the roaring sound returning to her ears. Groping her way to the small sofa, Roxanne leaned her head back to rest against the pillow and waited for him to return.

"Sorry to take so long but—hey!" Bram ran to the couch and pressed the back of his hands against her forehead and cheeks. Her skin was damp. "Roxanne?" He held his breath, his heart pounding furiously in his chest. *What if she had internal injuries? What if there was a brain trauma? What if—*

"I'm just resting," her eyes remained closed. "Really, I'm fine."

Relief left him momentarily exhausted. His eyes lingered on her features, visually caressing her high forehead, her softly rounded cheeks, and her pert nose before ending their tour on her slightly parted lips.

"What a shame." His tongue clicked against the roof of his mouth. "I was hoping I'd have to give you more mouth-to-mouth." Bram's lips moved closer to hers. "Although it might be just the thing to bring a little color to your complexion."

"Does my face need color?" Roxanne inquired without opening her eyes.

"Definitely."

"Be my guest."

The masculine lips that united with hers felt warm and wonderful. Roxanne supposed she could try to convince herself that the concussion was making her act the flirt. But that would be a lie. The truth was she needed to feel the security of Bram's arms around her, needed to feel the firm pressure of his mouth. Simply put, she needed Abraham Tyler.

Maybe there was something to the premise that danger heightened a person's senses, aroused them and inspired them to go beyond the norm. That's exactly what Roxanne knew she was doing—under normal conditions she would have never invited a man to kiss her.

I could do this every day for the rest of my life! Bram's subconscious made the startling declaration as his tongue gently trespassed into the moist recesses of her mouth. His hands caressed her bare shoulders and glided across the silken skin of her back.

From the beginning her looks had caught his eye, but he found his interest piqued by more subtle qualities of wit, warmth, sensitivity, and intellect. He had thought that two years ago when he had first met Roxanne Murdoch, and now his initial impression was confirmed.

The harem costume notwithstanding, Bram knew the woman was no fantasy. Roxanne was a person and he was beginning to be very conscious of the softly solid femaleness of her—too conscious and too soon. He knew he should let her go, but he didn't. He couldn't. So again and again his mouth joined with hers.

As Roxanne's hands moved from around Bram's neck to slide across his shoulders, her fingers discovered nubby terry cloth instead of the expected navy suiting. Dark lashes fluttering open, she broke the kiss and stared in amazement at his white tennis outfit. "Where in the world did this come from?"

A gentle forefinger tapped her nose. "That's what I came in here to tell you before I was so pleasantly interrupted." His knuckles caressed a blushing cheek. "Your color's back."

"You found the right prescription." She adroitly focused his attention back on his clothes. "Aren't those white shorts a bit presumptuous considering the weather?"

Bram grinned. "This outfit had every expectation of being out in the sun tomorrow morning getting in some practice with the new graphite racket waiting for me in St. Croix. But in lieu of that, and while my pants are drying out on the radiator in my office, they have been put into service." He reached on the table for his long-sleeve shirt. "I couldn't find a thing for you, but how about this?"

"Wonderful." Roxanne gratefully accepted the blue and white striped oxford-cloth dress shirt. "This costume is unbelievably itchy and I thank you much for this," she hugged his shirt. "But where were you hiding your tennis whites?"

"My briefcase," he explained. "I packed it and some grooming supplies to carry with me on the plane. On my last two business trips my luggage arrived the day I was leaving."

She shook her head. "From optimist to pessimist in one fell swoop."

"Pragmatist," he corrected her, and tossed her a pair of white socks. "Here, use these. Mine should be dry by now." Bram exhaled a regretful sigh as he watched Roxanne depart for the ladies' room. "You do realize your back view is almost as inspiring as your front," he called.

Roxanne paused in the doorway and looked back. "Just be grateful your colleagues didn't order a gorilla-gram. The guy that delivers them weighs two twenty and would need hours of mouth-to-mouth to bring up his color."

The fourth-floor powder room was comparable to a walk in a garden. Lush green carpeting spread underfoot like a grassy knoll and the trellised wallpaper was strewn with white daisy bouquets. But the fresh, springlike atmosphere changed the instant Roxanne's face was reflected in the mirror over the double sink.

Kohl-rimmed eyes with their dilated pupils looked like twin burnt holes embedded in her chalky complexion, and the white bandage stood prominently amid a wild disarray of brown curls. "And he actually kissed you, the Bride of Frankenstein!" Roxanne stuck her tongue out at her image.

After removing the last vestiges of her eye makeup and carefully reorganizing her hair, Roxanne relegated what was left of her costume to the trash container. Bram's shirt was a perfect fit, slightly long in the shoulders and sleeves, loose over her bare breasts with the shirttail hem stopping a little higher than mid-thigh to easily cover the sapphire blue leotard panty that covered her own apricot briefs.

With the addition of knee-high white tennis socks, Roxanne stared at her likeness in the full-length mirror behind the door. "I look ready for a teenage pajama party," she said, but the yawn she mockingly issued turned real and the slump to her posture was due to exhaustion compounded with an ever-increasing headache. She riffled the contents of her purse, found a tiny tin of aspirin, and washed three down with a paper cup of water.

Out in the hallway, she followed the sounds of a radio newscast to Bram's office. "Forty-mile-per-hour winds with gusts to sixty are combining with a still-falling fifteen inches of snow to reduce visibility to zero. A twenty-two-car pile-up has closed Interstate 94, leaving three dead and countless others seriously injured. Power outages and phone service has been lost, leaving one hundred thousand Twin Cities' residents without electricity. Schools and churches have opened their doors to shelter—"

"And to think we walked through all that!" Roxanne broke into the announcer's dissertation.

Bram looked to the doorway, then twisted the radio into silence. "I'd rather not think about it," he countered, and pushed himself out of his brown leather executive chair. "Can I get you anything? How's the head?"

"No to the first and okay to the second. I took some aspirin." She saw the tennis shorts had been replaced by his suit pants, and socks now covered his feet. Roxanne settled herself onto the small rust-tweed sofa that was centered against an oak-paneled wall, and tried to smother another yawn. "If you don't mind, I think I'll just curl up and sleep—"

"No." He was by her side in two long strides. "You can't sleep."

"Why not?"

"Because I read somewhere that people with head injuries should be kept awake."

Roxanne rolled her eyes toward the ceiling. "That's crazy. I'm tired. I want to sleep."

"That's your concussion talking," Bram insisted, settling next to her.

"Couldn't it just be because it's my normal bedtime, the fact that I've been up since six A.M. and trudged through the blizzard of the century?" came her smug retort.

"Huh!" was his only reply before he pulled her head down, lifted one end of the bandage, and examined the contusion. "At least it's stopped bleeding."

"Now can I sleep?" Her words were muffled against his chest.

"How about if I put the radio back on, find some music, and—"

"I won't dance, don't ask me." She yawned again and tried another tactic. "Why don't we make tonight our first date. Here we are, sitting on the sofa." Roxanne fluttered her lashes at him while her hands smoothed the wrinkles from the collar of his white tennis shirt. "I'll put my head here, and you can put your arm there." She was now comfortably ensconced in the curve of his shoulder. "And you can tell me all about your brothers and sisters and the small town where you were raised."

"I'm an only child who was raised in a city and I

know exactly what you're up to," he informed her in a succinct tone.

She ignored his innuendo. "Then tell me about your dog—the one that smells like my coat."

"You're going to fall asleep and use my body for a pillow."

"Only if your story's boring," Roxanne teased, then twisted her head to look at him. She found Bram was smiling. "Hasn't any woman ever used your body as her pillow?" Her eyes were wide and guileless.

His thumb and forefinger caught her chin. "Playing the coquette doesn't suit you, Roxanne Murdoch. You're too down-to-earth and honest." His palm curved around her neck, fingers encountering a thin gold chain. Bram pulled on the chain until a small gold medallion appeared. "Still wearing your harem jewelry?"

When she said nothing, he took a closer look at the relief motif on the circle. A gowned woman carrying shafts of wheat dominated one side and on the reverse was an astrology symbol and the name *Virgo*. "You're a horoscope believer."

"My aunt was an astrologer and had this struck for my eighteenth birthday," Roxanne explained. "She used to do charts for quite a few people, and I helped with the research. Astrology is two thousand years old and who knows—" Her eyebrows rose.

"Hmmm, I do find it rather interesting that since the fates have made me unable to get to the Virgin Islands tonight"—Bram paused to let the chain slowly shimmer down her throat to its original position—"they've at least had the decency to maroon me with a Celestial Virgin."

She gave him an impertinent grin. "I bet you're a Taurus—they make terrible lechers."

"April twenty-third."

"I was right. You're thoughtful, endearing, likable—"

Bram snapped his fingers. "Rats, and I so wanted to be a lecher!" Feeling her shiver, he asked, "Cold? The thermostats are locked in at sixty-eight. Maybe I can find something to use as a blanket." He reluctantly left his position to search for extra warmth.

Finding his topcoat still wet and her fur totally unapproachable, Bram climbed onto a chair in the lounge and took the heavy thermal-weave drapes off their rods. "I've found us a novel bedspread . . ." But his announcement fell on Roxanne's soundly sleeping form. For a long moment he indulged himself by staring at the shadowy female curves barely covered by his shirt, then he tucked the drapes around her before returning to the dining room to get the loose pillows on that small sofa and make himself a bed on the floor next to her.

Sometime during the night Roxanne became aware of a light being shined into her eyes. "What are you doing?" she mumbled sleepily.

Bram turned off the penlight. "Just checking my concussed patient. Warm enough?"

She snuggled farther into the sofa and under the covers. "Fine. What is this?"

"The drapes."

"A Taurus man is also a good provider."

CHAPTER FOUR

Her eyes still closed, Roxanne stretched her arms and legs from their nightlong fetal position on the small office sofa. As she struggled to sit up, the wide length of drapery fabric that pretended to be a coverlet shimmied to the floor. Seconds later a muffled voice hailed her. "Oops, sorry," Quickly she lifted the heavy beige thermal weave off Bram. "How are you doing down there?"

"Never mind me." His words were punctuated by yawns. "How are you? How's the head?" Not waiting for a reply, Bram was at her side, on his knees, and carefully lifting the gauze bandage for his inspection.

"My head feels fine," she announced. "The rest of me needs a chiropractor. This couch is a suitable bed only for a contortionist." Roxanne was growing more aware of the gentle fingers that ministered to her scalp. Fingers that began to play amid tousled curls rather than keeping to their doctoring duties.

69

She swallowed hard and tried to disguise her flustered reaction. "How's it look?"

With his hand still resting lightly against the right side of her head, Bram sat back on his heels. "Angry and still swollen. I should have remembered to put an ice pack on it last night." He failed in his attempt not to stare. The more he looked at her, the more beautiful she became, and the more he needed to look.

She was not a stunner who stopped conversations or made heads turn when she walked into a room, but her subdued, understated beauty had been on his mind and haunted his dreams all the night long. This morning Bram's eager eyes refused to leave her face.

Roxanne found herself blinking rapidly, trying to disconnect his mesmerizing gaze. "Ice pack! As I recall, my entire body was already below zero."

He drew his index finger slowly down her forehead to trace the arch of her eyebrow. Leaning his head close to hers, Bram inquired, "And how's your body temperature this morning?"

A fluttering of wings invaded her stomach, and Roxanne felt as if every nerve ending was exposed. "A perfect ninety-eight point six." The lie was spoken by suddenly sensitive lips.

She saw him smile, watched as he stood and stretched his lean physique, broad shoulders rippling awake beneath the white terry tennis shirt. It was then, in that one split-second, Roxanne ached to again feel his touch and to taste his mouth. She resolutely banished the ephemera and focused on something saner. "How about checking the weather," her too cheery voice invited as she swung herself off the sofa and straightened her shirt.

Bram went to the window and rolled up the autumn-toned roman shade.

When he didn't answer her persistent "How is it's," Roxanne moved to his side. Now there were two dumbstruck people staring in awe at the wild whiteness outside. Her hand curled around Bram's forearm. "Uh . . . try the radio."

The instant he pressed the power button the room filled with ear-grating static. "Odd, this is the same station we heard last night." Bram twisted the knob and sent the red indicator up the AM band, searching for a broadcast.

"Maybe you should try CONELRAD?"

He shook his head. "Roxanne, this is just a snowstorm not a nuclear holocaust. Besides, CONELRAD is extinct."

Brooding eyes looked out the window. "So may Minneapolis be! I have never seen anything like this."

"You're letting your imagination run crazy." Bram switched to the FM band and began repositioning the antenna. "Atmospheric conditions play havoc with radio waves." He slapped the side of the radio, moved it onto the window ledge, and tried the lower AM station numbers. Music interrupted the static. "See"—his reassuring smile appeased all of their fears—"the people at WCCO are on the job."

Roxanne sniffed, walked back to the sofa, and began to fold the drapes in a neat square while listening to Kenny Rogers's latest hit. Kenny was followed by a Glen Campbell golden oldie, a nonprescription diet pill advertisement, and a musical station identification jingle. Roxanne was just about to mumble some borderline obscenity when the announcer finally returned to the microphone.

"I'm back from the candy machine with my Hershey bar for breakfast," came a joking voice. "This is Russ Meyer with the nine thirty news and weather update. And if you've looked out the window, you'll see the weather is today's news. Normally I'm on the four-to-midnight shift here at WCCO, but thanks to Old Man Winter, I'm on overtime or is it double time?"

Bram groaned and thumped the radio. "Come on, buddy, give us the news."

"So far," Russ Meyer continued, "twenty-nine inches of snow has fallen on the Twin Cities and it's still coming, folks. A stalled low pressure system of unusual duration is bringing us snow and gale-to-hurricane force winds that have completely immobilized the city. Nothing is moving; nothing is open. Residents are instructed to stay where they are.

"Northern States Power reports an increase in power outages due to heavy wet snow and high winds downing power lines. Eleven new deaths have been reported due directly to the weather, bringing the total since yesterday at six to thirty-one.

"Will this rival the blizzard of eighty-eight when over fifty inches of snow blanketed the northeast in three days? In nine months will we record a baby boom with names of Snowflake, Snowdrift, and—"

Roxanne made a twisting motion with her fingers

and Bram snapped the jovial announcer into silence. "I hate someone that bright and bushy in the morning," she grumbled. "Damn, I've got too many things to do to stay here any longer."

"Be my guest." Bram made a carefree gesture. "Go outside and become a statistic. Roxanne Murdoch, the twelfth weather-related death."

"Oh, shut up." She went and sat on the edge of his desk, her leg swinging in random circles. "I'm just not civil before I've brushed my teeth and had a cup of coffee. Besides"—Roxanne glanced at him—"why are you in such a good mood? You're missing the sun and fun and tennis of St. Croix."

"But I was smart enough to take out vacation insurance," Bram grinned, his hand rasping along the dark stubble on his jaw. "Two days lost to the weather will not be lost to my wallet, and I still have twelve days to go." He walked around the desk and put both his hands on her shoulders. "Besides, both my shirt and I are having a wonderful time." His fingers took their time smoothing out the collar. "You look very good in men's clothes. I especially like your hat. Is it a hand-me-down from somebody special?"

Roxanne tried to remain as cool and civil about Abraham Tyler as she was about other men but found civility was the last thing on her mind. All those lustful thoughts that had to do with his lips and hands again invaded and corrupted her mind. And the giddy, dizzy feelings that kept drifting over her whenever he came close were so sophomoric. She was thirty, for heaven's sake!

Mentally Roxanne gave herself a hard slap while physically forcing her mouth to curve in a congenial smile. "It's a one-owner hat," she answered, trying to ignore the fact that his eyes matched the wide cobalt-blue stripe that banded the front of his sport shirt. "A spur-of-the-moment purchase to keep my head warm this winter."

"Well, that takes care of the hat." He kept his fingers on the very tips of the collar. "What about the somebody special?"

Her eyes narrowed against his persistent stare. "What about breakfast?" Roxanne adroitly changed the subject.

Bram slid a hand into his pocket and jingled some coins. "Does food put you in a more responsive mood?"

"Feed me breakfast and I might feed you some information," she parried. Since his hands had left her body, her emotions had stabilized and her normal equilibrium returned.

"This will be our second date," Bram reminded her in an easy banter, "and I'd hate to be infringing on someone else's territory."

"Territory?" Roxanne's eyes widened facetiously. "I'm not a piece of property that a man can buy and sell, Mr. Tyler. I hold my own deed and there is no mortgage that can be foreclosed."

His resonant laugh vibrated around the room. "Well, that answers my question."

"Do I still get breakfast?" Roxanne inquired, trying to keep her own amusement hidden. The main problem with Bram Tyler, she admitted silently, was the fact the man was incredibly likable.

"Breakfast and a toothbrush," Bram announced. At her questioning look his thumb jabbed toward the tan leather attaché case balanced across the wooden letter tray on his desk. "There's a travel kit inside filled with assorted hotel samples, soaps, toothpaste, and disposable razors. Plow through and help yourself." When Roxanne hesitated, he asked, "What's the matter?"

She wiggled uncomfortably on the desk. "A briefcase is . . . like a woman's purse. Sacred and private, untouchable by anyone but the owner. Maybe you better—"

"Honestly, Roxanne." He reached over and flipped up the unlocked lid and tossed her a brown nylon tote bag. "Is it just you, or are all Virgos this restrained?"

"Probably just me," she admitted, reluctantly pulling around the zipper. "Both my mother and my aunt instilled some very strict manners in me. To this day I ask permission to open my mother's refrigerator."

"You wait for permission? You, the successful, go-getting entrepreneur?" Bram shook his head. "Well, I can get that story over our luncheon date." He paused in the doorway to sort out various coins. "What do you want in your coffee? How about breakfast? There's a pastry machine, hard-boiled eggs, and yogurt in one of the others."

Roxanne looked up from sniffing a heavenly bar of jasmine-scented soap wrapped in white and bearing the imprint THE PLAZA, NEW YORK CITY. "Extra sugar and cream in the coffee," she instructed. She found a boxed toothbrush and mini-tube of Pepsodent marked FREE SAMPLE. "I'll take the egg and whole-wheat crackers with peanut butter."

Her fingers extracted a small silver box, the trademark emblazoned with red. "Oh, Bram," she caroled, her voice oddly melodic, "how long did you say your vacation was?"

"Two weeks." He put his hands together and showed off an impressive backhand with an invisible tennis racket. "Fourteen glorious sun-filled days in the Caribbean." He gave a philosophical shrug. "Now I'm down to an even dozen if I can get out of here tonight. Why?"

"Because I see you've packed something for those fun-filled nights as well." She held up a box of male contraceptives. "You have just enough for twelve various ladies du jour." Roxanne tossed him the tiny pack. "Nothing like carrying your heart in your briefcase."

Wincing, he deftly caught and pocketed the box. "What can I tell you. I was a Boy Scout and our motto is 'Be prepared.' Don't look so sanctimonious." Bram scowled at her expression. "I happen to think it's rather courteous and conscientious of me."

"And you're right," Roxanne agreed matter-of-factly. "You are courteous and conscientious. After all, you did give me the shirt off your back and all that mouth-to-mouth."

"You *aren't* civil till you've brushed your teeth

and had coffee," Bram admonished, his shoulders giving an exaggerated shiver before he exited the room.

The mirror in the powder room reflected a smile and an expression that changed from smug to respectful. Bram was being courteous and conscientious, Roxanne acknowledged while she displayed an assortment of toiletries on the metal shelf above the sinks. It was just a shock to her fastidious system to agree.

Fastidious? Her, the belly dancer! A fit of giggles interrupted the silence. But she was extremely fastidious when it came to sex. She hadn't indulged in free love in the seventies, wasn't ready for the sexual revolution of the eighties, and the thought of waking up next to a stranger made her physically ill. Yes, fastidious was a much nicer word than frigid!

The mirror now reflected a self-deprecating smirk. Richard had not actually called her frigid, just sexually undemonstrative, even after they'd become engaged and she'd finally succumbed to his inherent charm. Richard! Roxanne frowned. Now, why had Richard Beck popped into her mind?

Maybe it was natural for a woman to compare the new man she's just met with a man she's always tried to forget. But Abraham Tyler and Richard Beck were complete opposites. Bram had black hair and mature, rugged features while Richard was blond with a little boy's face that could harden like concrete in an expression of disapproval. Bram was fun and easy-going and Richard—well, Richard was the epitome of a stuffed shirt. Roxanne giggled again.

Richard should have been a banker rather than an office manager. He'd fit in so well with the marbled floors and the monotonous decor.

Brown eyes scrutinized her image. She had been extremely sensible about falling in love with Richard. He was what every mother wished for her daughter. Kind, respectful, good job, headed for advancement, no vices, no hidden quirks. And Roxanne had tried to be what every mother wished for their son. Well-mannered, proper, obedient, sweet, loving. But she'd found being something you weren't made her terribly depressed and slightly insane. So she took off her disguise and became herself, and then she introduced Richard to Aunt Mathilda.

Aunt Mathilda hadn't liked Richard. Sweaty upper lip, damp palms, and a smile that never reached his hazel eyes. Aunt Mathilda had been right! Richard had a fit when she'd told him about starting Greetings and Salutations. His future wife dressed in those outrageous costumes, doing equally outrageous skits! Never! Roxanne had to make a choice—her business venture or her future spouse.

The business won and so Roxanne realized, after two months of mourning and moping, had she. She was not meant to be Mr. Richard Beck's better half. In fact at the age of twenty-five she realized she wasn't mentally and emotionally ready to be anyone's Mrs.

She had set her priorities five years ago and men had not even made the list. After Richard, she knew what she wanted in a man; she didn't need to experiment. She'd know Mr. Right when he came along.

Quite truthfully, she wasn't upset or miserable without a man in her life. She didn't feel worthless or depressed or sterile. She felt quite well.

As she began to unbutton the oxford-cloth shirt, Abraham Tyler's face loomed with three-dimensional accuracy in her mind and again an unfamiliar strangeness washed over her. Roxanne knew she liked him, but then she liked and was a platonic friend to four other men whom she'd known for over a decade.

But none of those men ever made you feel anxious, her subconscious cautioned her. *Even Richard never made you feel prickly.*

Roxanne unwrapped the hotel soap and worked it into a rich lather in the hot-water-filled basin. "Anxious." Saying the word out loud made her feel less. "Probably just the concussion." She wreathed her face in iridescent bubbles. "Just the concussion." Her words blended into a musical humming that soon turned into a song.

Bram had just finished rinsing his disposable razor for the last time when the melody of Gershwin's *American in Paris* drifted through the adjoining bathroom wall followed by Irving Berlin's *Say It with Music.* Grinning, he squirted some aftershave into his palm from the tiny plastic bottle marked SAMPLE, NOT FOR SALE. Roxanne really had a lovely voice, but her choice of songs were a mystery.

Usually a person sang one of the top ten records or even a year-old favorite, but the Gershwin and Berlin tunes would be current only if this were 1923 —the same year her coat had been in vogue. The lady

79

was very intriguing. An independent, bright, brash business woman tempered by old-fashioned manners and the ability to blush. Contradictory and complex, and he appreciated her more with every passing minute.

Pulling his shirt over his head, Bram brushed down his thick hair, noting the addition of a few more gray strands at the temples. He had been feeling rather old lately, old and cynical and moody. That had been the reason for his two-week vacation. A little rejuvenation under the swaying palms and the tropical sun. *Old Man River* was now being crooned by his companion, and Bram watched his smile broaden in the mirror.

He wasn't feeling old and stodgy this morning despite the weather and the confinement. Or maybe it was because of it. Maybe, Bram mused with due consideration, he'd just keep hoping the weather outside would remain frightful, because he was certainly feeling delightful. His deep voice hummed, "Let it snow, let it snow, let it snow."

Bram had just placed a container of steaming coffee on her side of the dining table when Roxanne walked into the lounge. "Perfect timing," he said with a smile. "Breakfast is served." He saw her eye him warily when he moved to pull out her chair. "Just trying to put you in a civil mood."

"Before you ply me with questions?" She took hesitant sips of the hot liquid before opening the package of crackers.

"All the better to know you, my dear Roxanne. Here we are, alone, together, just the two of us."

80

When his eyebrows bounced up and down, she choked on a laugh. "You make such a lousy big bad wolf."

He pouted. "And you're not scared of me at all?"

"Not a bit." Roxanne rolled the egg along the Formica tabletop, listening to the shell crackle. "My aunt taught me to handle big bad wolves."

"Ah, the aunt again." Bram opened a carton of pineapple yogurt. "You know these professional spinster aunts can be detrimental to a young woman's emotional health."

"What makes you think she was a spinster?"

"Was she?"

Roxanne shook salt on top of her egg before answering. "Yes. As a matter of fact, Aunt Mathilda was fond of saying she never found a reason to marry."

His index finger stabbed the air. "What did I tell you! I bet she brainwashed you in other matters as well."

"Brainwashed is rather a strong word," she returned with due consideration. "Let's just say—"

"Brainwashed," Bram interrupted. "I minored in psychology. It's important for a banker, especially a loan officer, to be able to read people."

She digested both his statement and the egg. "Yes, I suppose it is. Are you always right?"

The plastic spoon clattered against the empty container. "Always," he related proudly. "Now tell me about you and your family and"—Bram ripped open the plastic wrap on an apple danish—"especially Aunt Mathilda."

Roxanne sprinkled more salt on the egg yolk while taking time to sort through her thoughts. She could feel Bram watching her every move, every expression. When she lifted her face on level with his, she made sure her features were impassive. "Well, you already know about my two sets of twin brothers and that I'm from Chicago."

His dark head nodded with eager enthusiasm. "And how did you land in Minneapolis?"

"Aunt Mathilda." Roxanne ignored his "Ahhha" and continued. "She was twenty years older than my mother and just after I graduated from high school, Aunt had an accident, broke her hip, and was confined to a wheelchair. Since there were equally good business colleges here, I relocated and moved in with her. She passed away three years ago at the age of eighty-one."

"Isn't that just about the time you broke free and created your greeting service?"

"Actually I *broke free* two years before," she corrected him, taking a swallow of coffee. "I'd worked in a business office for five years and found unmarried women are considered 'girls' while unmarried men were 'colleagues.'" Her stoic expression faded as a roughness entered her voice. "Every time I tried to move up in the office ranks, a less qualified male coworker got the title and the salary and the perks while I got his workload. So I decided I'd have a lot more zest for life if I ran my own business rather than play the lackey for someone else's. I knew my business wouldn't fail due to poor management."

"Of course," Bram persevered, "it could have all

been tied to a subconscious effort on your part to be free of your aunt and your confining nursing duties. I bet you used to help your mother with the twins, right?"

"Yes, so?"

He lifted his hand. "First a babysitter-nurse at fifteen, then jumping right into another health-care situation from eighteen to what? Twenty-four? Twenty-five?" When he saw her lips twist, Bram pounced. "See what I mean. You were going through all the motions but not really living. And when you started Greetings, you exploded; all that pent-up energy and emotion just waiting to be expressed. Yet you still felt safe because of the costumes and masks."

"Hmmm. I never looked at it that way, but then *I* don't have a minor in psychology."

So intent on knowing her every thought, Bram failed to notice her sarcastic undertone. "Does that bother you? Not having a college degree?"

Roxanne was startled for a moment. "No. I find that a social education is much more rounding and useful. Working in an office is quite an education; personalities abound and you grow up very fast."

"Did someone make you grow up too fast?" His deep voice grew persuasive. "Is that why you're so committed to your business?"

"What makes you think that?" She bristled and stuffed assorted paper garbage into the empty cup.

Bram leaned back in the chair, arms folded across his chest. His eyes never left her face. "Call it a sixth sense."

"First a photographic memory, then a psychologist, now a psychic. My, my, Mr. Tyler, you certainly run the gamut."

"Now, now," he smiled, "would you like another coffee? I think you're losing your civility."

Roxanne's jaw dropped. "Losing my civility!" When she began to sputter, she stopped, took a deep breath, counted to ten, and tried to ignore his broad grin. "I just don't happen to appreciate the ease with which you make assumptions."

He spread his hands. "I make my assumptions on facts." He ticked off each pronouncement on a finger. "You're very protective of your business, yet you haven't even asked to use the phone to call anyone to tell them you're here. The hat was not a hand-me-down, and finally your little speech about holding your own deed said a lot. I'll wager you had a very serious commitment going and Aunt Mathilda soured you on the guy and you ended it."

A sweep of dark lashes shielded the sparkle in Roxanne's eyes. "You are amazing," she admitted at last. "I did have a serious commitment. Aunt didn't like him and I did end it." When she looked at him, her gaze was calculated. "I wonder what Aunt would have thought of you?"

Bram leaned across the table, his fingers splayed on either side of her face. "You wouldn't have cared. You wouldn't have even asked." His manner was bold, his tone slightly hoarse. "I would have made sure you were positive about me, positive about us, positive about love. Nothing and no one would have mattered."

Roxanne could sense a change in Bram's mood. He seemed urgent, almost hungry. His face kept moving closer until it blocked out everything else. Her own breathing became erratic. Her moist palms gripped the edge of the table. If she didn't do something fast, he was going to kiss her. And if Bram did kiss her, she knew she'd kiss him back. Then there was no telling what would happen next. She was feeling anxious again, so Roxanne mentioned his mother.

His head jerked back. "I . . . I beg your pardon?"

"I said"—she gave an inward sigh of relief when he sat back down—"I bet your mother had a lot to do with making you feel so confident and secure."

"Yes, I suppose she did. She and my father were always supportive. I lost them both when I was nineteen," he told her, his voice growing wistful. "But they were always with me in spirit and so were their values."

She reacted with pleasure. "What a lovely thing to say and how rare. I hear so many people blaming their parents for everything that's wrong in their lives." Roxanne found she was curious to learn more. "Tell me what happened to Bram Tyler at the age of nineteen?"

"I moved in with Uncle Sam aboard an aircraft carrier for four years, came back home to Minnesota, got a master's degree in business, and followed in my father's footsteps in a banking career."

"And what about all the women who helped you grow up?" It was her turn to be persistent and annoying.

"There have been a few rather intense relationships," he confided easily. "But ultimately I knew they weren't quite right and—" Bram made a dismissing gesture.

Roxanne exhaled an unladylike snort. "Rather insensitive of you."

"It'd be worse to lead a woman on," he was quick to point out. "Over the years you mature enough to distinguish between desire and love. You search for someone who lights fires in your heart, not just in your . . . libido."

Again Roxanne found it necessary to lower her eyes from the intensity of his gaze. She eagerly looked for a savior and found it in the wall clock. "Why don't you go check with that radio announcer; the news will be on in a minute and we might get a more favorable weather report. Maybe you'll be sipping a piña colada at midnight in St. Croix."

She literally collapsed farther into the chair when he ambled out of the lounge. Every muscle in her body was tight and tense. *How silly,* Roxanne rationalized, *all the man was planning to do was kiss me. And I have been kissed before. And kissed by him!*

That was the crux of her fears. Bram Tyler certainly knew how to kiss. Her tongue slowly swept her lips, the moistness and pressure reminding her of his warm, wonderful mouth. How incredibly easy it had been to lose herself in his arms. Lose herself.

A shiver coursed down her spine; she didn't want to ever lose Roxanne Murdoch again. She was happy and content with herself and remembered how awful it was to pretend to be someone else. Pushing herself out of the chair, Roxanne walked to the undraped window and stared out at the still-raging storm. "Damn it, Mother Nature, can't you take a break so I can get out of here before—" She hesitated a moment, and then refused to finish the sentence.

CHAPTER FIVE

Bram stood quietly in the doorway of the lounge just savoring the sight of her. Roxanne was seated sideways on a chair, her face and upper body concealed by yesterday's newspaper. Her long legs were displayed to their best advantage—crossed at the knee, the shirt hem curled back to expose a sleek length of thigh while the white cotton tennis socks conformed to shapely calves.

Dancer's legs, his appreciative brain asserted. Long from hip to knee and from knee to ankle. Ankles that looked delicate but were strong, and feet that were agile. Bram remembered how inviting those legs looked among the sapphire silk panels of the harem costume. Inviting and tempting and teasing and tormenting.

Fifty percent of him wanted to feel those legs wrapped tightly around him, while the other half yearned to explore, sample, and master the rest of her soft feminine terrain. *Master?* Bram frowned. No, he didn't want to master or conquer Roxanne.

He wanted to share with her the loving communication between their two bodies.

His right hand moved to rub the tension from his neck. Funny, he'd never been so instantly passionate about a woman before. He was not acting with his usual rationale. Maybe his reactions were just the result of the accident and their adventure. Maybe all this was just adolescent infatuation and it would disappear like the twenty-four-hour flu. Probably the best thing he could do was just relax and be more logical about it.

Roxanne turned the page and saw Bram standing next to the door. She lowered the paper and inquired, "Well, what's the verdict? Do we get a paroled from the Hepworth Hilton?"

"Let me put it to you this way," he recounted, walking into the room and tossing two magazines on the table, "there is now three feet of snow and it's still falling, wind chill factor reported at forty-five below, more power outages, nothing is out, not plows, sanders, police, burglars or—"

Roxanne held up her hand. "No more," she begged. "I get the picture." Her gaze strayed to the table. "Great, you found some new reading material." She neatly folded the third-time-read *Tribune* and reached for *Fortune* magazine. "This looks interesting. I liked that banking magazine." An hand waved abstractedly toward the end table. "Some very good articles," she muttered, becoming more involved with the printed page.

Bram dispelled a capitulative sigh, purchased a carton of milk, and settled on the padded window seat with his secretary's well-thumbed issue of *Cosmopolitan.*

When a continual series of *ahhs* and *ohhs* kept interrupting her reading, Roxanne held back as long as possible before verbally walking into what she instinctively knew was a trap. "All right, you've got my attention. What are you reading that's so exciting?"

"An article about you."

Wide sable eyes narrowed to mink-brown slits as they watched Bram's mouth curve into an attractive smile. "Me? I just know I'm stepping into quicksand but—" Her hand fluttered for an explanation.

"The Cosmo Girl's Bedside Astrologer." He held up a colorful insert. "Everything a man should know about a Virgo personality but is afraid to ask."

"Those things are written to fit two million readers," Roxanne jeered. "They're totally inaccurate. To do an astral casting properly, you have to know the exact time and date a person was born and the position of the planets in relation to both the earth and the stars," she told him. "You are not reading a valid horoscope."

His thumb scratched a lean cheek. "Then none of this is true to you?"

"Extremely doubtful."

"You wouldn't mind if I just asked you a few questions to check all this out?"

Roxanne sighed. "Could I stop you?" When he shook his head she rolled her eyes. "Go ahead."

Bram cleared his throat. "Your ruling planet?"

"Mercury."

"Favorite color?"

Her fingernails tapped impatiently across the Formica tabletop. "Well, I really have two—brown and black."

He looked disappointed. "It says here primrose yellow." A suspicious light entered his eyes. "Say, you haven't read this already and—"

"No, I haven't," Roxanne shot back. "Yellow makes me look jaundiced. I have never owned anything yellow. See, what did I tell you—generalizations." She turned back to her magazine.

"Now, wait a minute," Bram protested. "Do a few more. Ah-ha! Well, this one is right. It says your best features are your full womanly bosom and showgirl legs." When she just grunted, he continued. "You are also methodical, exact, efficient, and an industrious, dependable worker. Quiet, reliable, disciplined, and tidy. Good sense of humor."

"That . . . that's true," she related grudgingly. "Saturn, which is a disciplined planet, is located in my first house, the house of physical appearance and personality. I am a tidy person."

"I noticed how spic-and-span the lounge was when I came back." His dark head nodded in agreement. "And I can vouch for your quick wit. Let's see now, where was I . . . oh, yes. Health: You face each day in the best frame of mind only when you've had plenty of sleep the night before. Fortune: your business success is riding high and your talent for turning clever ideas in cold cash is paying off. Beauty: the sun is your worst enemy and you might consider having those puffy bedroom eyes taken care of."

"Puffy bedroom eyes! Of all the nerve," she bristled, a gentle finger stroking the insulted area.

"*You* said these were generalities," Bram reminded her. "Oh-oh, here's a good one under adventure—you'll soon enjoy an excursion in the great outdoors."

Roxanne gave a self-conscious laugh. "That was on target. We did have an outdoor excursion, but I'm more of an indoor sport."

. "Hmmm, indoor sport." He made an intense study of the printed page. "Yes, there are a few notations here on the indoor Virgo. All sorts of men are captivated by your charm, but you are the zodiac's choosiest sign and never bestow affections lightly. But your love life, which has been stagnant of late, finds itself solidly in *amour.*"

. *Stagnant, how well put!* She sucked in her cheeks. "Another generality."

"Favorite romantic rendezvous: in front of the fire on your fur coat and"—Bram paused a moment for effect—"in the office, late at night. Virgo's erogenous zones: sensitive nipples." He watched twin spots of color stain her cheeks. "And the tender backs of your knees."

Roxanne was feeling anxious again. "The backs of my knees?" She stood up and neatly pushed the chair under the table. "The next time the schnauzer who lives across the street nuzzles the backs of my knees I'll have to remember to swoon with passion." She folded her arms across her chest. "What does it say about Taurus?"

He licked his thumb and turned the page. "Astral

attractions . . . Taurus. Well, this is nice." Bram gave her a winning smile. "I'm prudent and thoughtful. Thrifty, sexually sensitive, determined, and my Boy Scout virtues appeal to you."

"Oh, yes, your Boy Scout virtues." Her tone was sarcastic. "As I remember, they were all neatly packaged in your briefcase."

He made a clucking noise with his tongue. "It must be time to feed you again; you're becoming uncivil."

"Then I shall take my uncivil self to the powder room and rebrush my teeth." Roxanne scooped up her purse and made a dignified exit despite the accompaniment of Bram's laughter.

Fifteen minutes later the ladies' room door reverberated under an imperative barrage. Roxanne moved away from the mirror where she'd been checking her eyes to open the door. "You knocked?"

Bram looked at her expression and made a face. "Come on, where's that Virgo sense of humor?"

"I'm in here sharpening it."

"I'm lonesome." The instant his fingers circled her wrist he felt a sense of relief. Roxanne was like a moving target and Bram was becoming more and more obsessed with catching her. "Besides——" He gave her arm a gentle tug. "I ran out of quarters; you'll have to spring for lunch." Her airy laugh was like a tonic to his senses.

Searching her coat pockets and the bottom of her purse, Roxanne discovered a mountain of coins and a half dozen rumpled dollar bills that the change machine efficiently converted to usable currency. A repast of ham salad sandwiches, milk, potato chips, and cookies littered the dining table.

"Our third date and I'm letting you buy the lunch." Bram opened his second milk carton. "You can't say I'm not liberal-minded."

Roxanne shook out the last of the chips. "Why do I get the distinct impression you're enjoying our imprisonment?" When he merely grinned, she wrinkled her nose. "Did you check on the weather report?"

He swallowed and nodded. "You're lucky to be imprisoned in a heated building," Bram admonished. "Your end of town just lost power." At her muttered "Wonderful" he commented: "I find it very interesting that you live in a house."

"I like the freedom a house affords," Roxanne confided. "I'm not an apartment person. The sound of other people's footsteps over my head and conversations all around me make me feel crowded." She licked the salt off her fingers. "I will confess I was surprised to discover my aunt willed me her home."

"Aunt Mathilda again. I should have guessed." He gave a disgusted snort. "That old spinster is still controlling your life from her grave. I bet that house looks just like her and I bet that you haven't removed one speck of her furnishings."

Roxanne watched her fingers play with the white plastic straw. "You are amazing. My respect for your psychological renderings grows every minute." Guileless chestnut eyes lifted to gaze intently on his face. "I'd be interested to hear what you think my *home* looks like."

It took Bram only a minute to visualize her surroundings. "I know from the address that it's in a older neighborhood. Probably a pre–World War II bungalow filled with stiff horsehair-covered Victorian furniture, crocheted antimacassars and doilies, Tiffany lamps, maybe a Spanish fan on display—"

"Psychic!" Roxanne's hand slapped her chest as she leaned against the back of her chair. "You not only pinpointed the architecture but even the fans." Her fingers ruffled through her soft brown curls. "You know, Bram, maybe you should go back and take some graduate courses in psychology. You're just too good at reading people."

She watched him preen like a peacock, but when he started bombarding her with more of his psychological hoopla, Roxanne knew she'd better change the subject or she'd burst his bubble and tell him the truth. "What about you?" she interrupted. "Tell me where you live."

"Hawk Ridge in Edina," came his easy answer. "I just moved into a very nice town house complex not far from the country club. It's a self-contained community nestled in the trees—security checkpoints, groundskeepers, health spa, pool, and tennis courts."

"And your house," she pressed, "I bet it's wall-to-wall bookcases, an oversize recliner chair, modular sofa—"

"Now, who's psychic!" Bram opened the package of Oreos and passed her two. "I purchased a model. The color choices and wallpapering had all been done by a professional decorator and, to be honest, I just reduplicated some of the furniture."

He swallowed in discomfort as Roxanne twisted

her cookie apart and the tip of her pink tongue slowly licked the white frosting in the center. Didn't she realize the effect her actions was having on his body? When he took a vicious bite out of his Oreo, his teeth caught the side of his cheek and the ensuing pain gelded his libidinous thoughts.

"Did you say something?" Roxanne asked.

"I—I—" Bram groped for a coherent lie. "I wondered how you liked living alone in that museum of a house?"

Poor Aunt Mathilda. She gave an inward grimace. *She's probably rolling in her grave and aching to smite this man. All in due time, Auntie. . . . All in due time.* "Dusting and fluffing all the doilies does take up all my free time," Roxanne returned sweetly. "But I do enjoy living alone. I'm not afraid, if that's what you're driving at. As a matter of fact, I became a crime statistic two years ago. I got mugged and—"

"Mugged!" His last cookie crumbled amid clenching fingers. "My God, what happened? Did you get hurt? Who did it? I'd like to get my hands around his neck and—"

Roxanne was astonished by Bram's protective reaction. There was no denying the honesty of the man's feelings. "Whoa." Her palm moved to cover his fist, her fingertips making soothing circles against his wrist. "I wasn't hurt. Not even touched." A giggle escaped her lips. "But the mugger—that poor kid probably still limps and talks one octave higher."

He inhaled sharply. "You mean you mugged the mugger?"

She nodded and smiled. "He was a pretty stupid

96

mugger," Roxanne related. "At least four inches shorter than I am, he had to jump up to put his knife near my throat and—"

"Knife!" Bram closed his eyes. "He was armed and you . . . you could have been killed." His eyes quickly opened, not enjoying the little vignette his subconscious was playing. "What did your parents say? And your aunt. I'm surprised she didn't ship you back to Chicago."

Sighing, she began to clean the table. "I didn't tell anyone because they'd have had the same reaction you're having. Nothing happened. I was fine; he wasn't. He disappeared into the night; I went home and wallowed in a bubble bath for two hours." Roxanne stuffed the garbage into the waste container. "I'll admit it took me a few days to realize the enormity of what could have happened"—she ignored his mumbled interruption—"so I took another self-defense course at the Y and bought a Mace cannister."

"I really think—"

Roxanne waved him silent. "Look, a friend of mine visited New York City, Miami, L.A., and Chicago and was never bothered, and then she went back home to visit her parents in Waterbury, Vermont, and had her purse snatched in the supermarket. Crime is everywhere and, yes, it is a drawback to living in the city," she agreed, "but it's a subjective intimidation and working and living in this complicated environment is stimulating and vital and increases a person's self-reliance." Brown eyes challenged blue. "I don't intend to move. I like living alone in my house. I'm not afraid. End of discussion. Do you play gin rummy or two-handed bridge?"

Bram blinked. "What?"

"While I was cleaning up after breakfast I found a deck of cards." She opened the cabinet door and took out a black plastic box. "Since we've exhausted all the personal conversations for one day," came her emphatic statement, "I thought we could amuse ourselves with gin or bridge."

"No Old Maid."

"Keep it up, Tyler," she threatened, "and you'll be playing fifty-two pick-up."

His palms rose in surrender. "Okay, okay," Bram laughed. "Gin it is. But I'm giving you fair warning." He rubbed his hands together. "I'm a whiz at any card game. I plan to clean out the Caribbean casinos."

"Banker, psychologist, psychic, and now wizard. Why, Bram Tyler"—her lashes fluttered like delicate wings as she settled in her chair—"you are just too good to be true."

"What can I say?" He reached for the box, tapped out the cards, and expertly began to shuffle. "Modesty becomes me." Bram's own laughter mingled with hers. "Listen, you wouldn't like to make this game a little more interesting? Say ten cents a point."

"Oh, I . . ."

"How about a penny a point?" He neatened the deck for her to cut. "Or is that still too rich for you? I wouldn't dream of taking advantage of you, considering your concussion and all."

Her fingernails tapped the cards in approval. "My

head never felt clearer and a dime a point sounds just fine."

Bram quickly dealt ten cards each and placed the twenty-first card face-up beside the remaining deck. "I bet you used to play cards with your aunt." He checked her discard before drawing his own.

"Yes, we did. Auntie was fond of saying it kept her off the streets," Roxanne noted, arranging and sorting her game suits. "How about you? Or perhaps you have an Aunt Mathilda of your own?"

"I played regular Sunday-afternoon games with my grandfather while he'd tell me all about the good old days." He tossed out the three of diamonds. "Gramps would have enjoyed your singing this morning."

Roxanne's hand hovered over his discard. "Singing? Was I singing?" She picked up the two cards.

"Yes, and very lovely too, but your songs were over sixty years old. Auntie's influence again." He drew another diamond but remembering what she'd picked up, discarded a heart. "She made you live in a time warp."

"The time warp served me well," she parried. "When I first started Greetings, singing telegrams were my biggest bookings," Roxanne countered, smiling as he winced when she took the discarded heart. "And most people requested old songs, which was perfect, because I knew them all." She looked up from her hand, her eyes glittering and announced: "Gin," and laid down perfect diamond and heart melds, discarding a spade.

Her laughter blotted out Bram's grumbling. "I get

an extra twenty-five points for going gin plus . . ." She quickly added up his total points. "Oh, my, you have three aces, that's fifteen points each, five picture cards and, hmmm, that totals one hundred thirty-five points times ten cents each . . . hmmm . . ." Roxanne pondered her newfound wealth. "If this is how you play cards, wizard, perhaps we should discuss your credit rating and collateral."

"Oh, shut up and deal! This is only the first game, lady," Bram pointed out with gruff determination. "Don't start investing your ill-gotten gains yet."

Microwaved hot dogs, chicken soup, cheese crackers and M&M's comprised dinner, eaten between cut-throat hands of gin rummy. By midnight they were both waking each other to take their corresponding turns.

Losing yet another game, Bram threw his cards on the table in disgust. "I'm cheating and I can't even win."

"Cheaters never prosper," Roxanne reminded him. She found it difficult to total the points mentally. "I'm beat. The Hepworth Casino is officially closed for the night."

Bram stretched, yawned, and rubbed a large hand over his face, his beard stubble scratching his palm. "How much do I owe you, Shylock?"

"Four hundred fifty-three dollars and ten cents." She followed him out of the lounge to his office. "Take heart—gambling losses are tax deductible." Roxanne shivered. "Is it getting colder, or is it me?"

He checked the thermostat on the wall, tapped the glass cover, and frowned. "It's dropped to fifty-eight.

The furnace must not be able to keep up against the outside temperature. Maybe I'd better check the radio again."

"Don't bother, Bram. We'll only feel that much colder." She stared at the two-seater couch with dispassionate eyes. "I'm going to make the supreme sacrifice—you get the sofa, I'll take the floor and the cushions."

"That's very chivalrous of you, but no thanks, I wouldn't dream of putting you out. Besides, you looked so cute all hunched up in a ball this morning."

Roxanne stuck out her tongue. She tugged the cushion backs and found they were stationary, but the seats were two loose units. "How about if we add these two to the four you have and take three cushions each? I'll let you share the drapery bedspread."

"Deal." But while Bram helped her coordinate the pillows into a makeshift bed, he wondered just how much sleep he was going to get with her lying next to him. Talk about a double-edged sword. Feeling at once aroused and self-condemning, he snapped off the desk light and stumbled his way onto the floor bed.

At first he had his back to her but decided that was rather ill-mannered and rude. Bram contemplated turning on his right side, toward her, and wondered if that wouldn't be considered bold and presumptuous. The solution to his problem was to lie on his back.

"Is this your regular bedtime exercise program?" Roxanne asked interestedly. "Or are you uncomfortable sleeping with someone?" Her narrowed gaze sought his finally stable profile in the darkness.

"These are the exercises I do when I'm sleeping *next* to someone. I'm much more athletic when I'm sleeping *with* someone." Bram turned his head, his teeth flashing in wolfish appeal. He smiled when he heard her laugh. "Of course, with you I'm very conscious of all those prim and proper thoughts Aunt Mathilda brainwashed into you."

"Please, no more references to Auntie. Let's move onto a safer subject." She was quiet a second. "How about your grandfather?"

"Interesting the way you divert me by asking about one of my relatives." When she made no response, Bram sighed and stared at the ceiling. "He was a banker too. My father succeeded him as president of the Cardiff Bank that merged with Hepworth."

"So you're truly the chip off the banker's block. That's nice."

Bram yawned in agreement. "What about your brothers? Isn't any one of them interested in following in your father's footsteps?" He turned his head toward her. "What does your father do? And your mother? I'm absolutely positive good old Aunt Mathilda was a schoolteacher who punctuated each lesson with a cat-o'-nine-tails."

Roxanne formed her answer very carefully. "My mother has a full-time job raising four teenage boys what with food, laundry, car pools, soccer, baseball . . . and my brothers keep changing their minds and fighting over who's going into outer space first."

"And your dad?" His words slurred and he was having a difficult time keeping his eyes open.

"Just retired. He's having fun puttering in the garden, fishing, doing some freelance consulting." Hearing Bram's "Mmmm" and noting the steadiness of his breathing, Roxanne relaxed and said no more.

Without the shield of conversation she became vividly aware of the storm. Frozen snow fiercely pelted the window while violent gusts of wind rattled across the building's architecture. Pulling the heavy drape to her chin, Roxanne snuggled deeper into the cushions, closed her eyes, and tried to sleep.

Sleep proved elusive under her ever-growing awareness of the warm, vital man lying beside her. She came up on one elbow and looked down at Bram. Her eyes had grown accustomed to their shrouded surroundings and she found a teenager's silliness engulf her as she uninhibitedly stared at his face.

She took each feature apart, hoping to find something not to like, anything that she could use to dissipate the feelings that were increasing in intensity with every passing second. The longer Roxanne looked, the more pleasurably her senses reacted to such attractive stimuli.

Carefully, and just above his skin, her index finger followed the strong line of his determined jaw to hover over his well-shaped mouth before tracing the curve of his cheek. She liked his wide forehead and the rugged dark brows that sheltered his deep blue eyes. Her fingers lifted a truant lock of hair that fell against his forehead. The blue-black strands distinguished by a few steel gray ones were thick against her fingertips.

Distinguished. The perfect word to describe Abraham Tyler, seventh vice president of the Hepworth National Bank. Abraham Tyler, a man descended from a long line of bankers. Roxanne shivered again, but the temperature wasn't the contributing factor, anxiety was. She wished she hadn't asked about his family; she wished she'd remained cool and aloof and disinterested.

The more intimate knowledge she had on this man, the more she liked him and the more confused she felt. How did she ever get into this position? She had a nice, quiet, orderly, sensible life and didn't need a trespasser. Her business commitment came above emotional entanglements. She'd had no regrets about that until yesterday—until she'd become better acquainted with Bram Tyler.

Bram sniffled and twisted in sleep; his snoring became more pronounced. Roxanne found herself smiling at the guttural, masculine sounds. He breathed in and out noisily. In and out. In and out. In and . . . she waited expectantly but didn't hear him complete the cycle. Fear clutched her, she'd read reports about men dying in their sleep from snoring.

She lifted his eyelid, heard him gurgle, choke, and sputter. Then suddenly she found herself pinned beneath his powerful body, her arms floundering limply around his neck. "I save the man's life and he crushes me."

"Save me? You scared me to death."

"The feeling was mutual, sir. I thought you had snored yourself into the world beyond."

He winced and shifted slightly but did not free her. "Sorry about that. Didn't mean to wake you up."

"It's not your fault. It's your nose. Too small for proper breathing and—"

"I didn't realize you had a nose fetish!" Bram lowered his head, letting his nose rub against hers. "You've insulted it for the last time, fair Roxanne." His voice deepened. "I'll be glad to show you the size of my nose is totally disproportional to the length of my—"

"I believe you," came her hasty acknowledgment. "Now, why don't you and your nose roll over and start snoring again."

Bram shook his head. "I don't think so. I like this position so much better." His hand made a slow journey from her shoulder to her breast. "In fact, this seems to be the perfect time to check out your erogenous zones." Capable fingers stroked the slumbering soft nipple into alert hardness. "Looks like that astrological guide is right on target."

Roxanne tried to dismiss the serenely spreading warmth that threatened her equilibrium. "You've an unfair advantage. I don't know your erogenous zones."

His lips nuzzled along the curve of her jaw. "Surprisingly enough, where you're concerned it's my eyes and my brain," Bram admitted before pressing a flurry of kisses in the scented hollow of her throat. "You've been visually and mentally caressing me since we first met and I've been thriving on it." He unfastened her shirt button. "I couldn't have ordered a more perfect woman."

The husky voice that delivered those words and Bram's slow, deliberate touch stealthily mesmerized Roxanne. His mouth charted a sensuous course over the velvety swell of her breasts, his lips eagerly pressing urgent kisses against her tingling flesh. A low, pleasurable moan escaped her throat the instant his tongue began to draw tantalizing circles around the hardened peak.

"Bram, please . . ." The palms that pressed into his biceps had meant to push him away and restore her freedom. Instead, Roxanne found her hands ached to explore his firm, athletic body, her fingers intrigued by the sinewy muscles in his shoulders and back.

"Mmmm . . . I was wrong," he breathed, nuzzling his face between the soft pillows of her full breasts, "having you touch me is so much more gratifying than just looking at you." His mouth hungered for hers, swooping to capture and savor her lips. His purposeful tongue gained easy access into the honeyed sweetness beyond and discovered an ardent mate.

Roxanne couldn't seem to get close enough to him. Her fingers splayed through his thick hair, demanding that his mouth not break contact with hers. His excitement fed her own, releasing a wild, abandoned side that she had never known. Where their bodies touched, at the shoulders, hips, and thighs, heat raged. Blood percolated in her veins, making her feel like she'd been infused with fire.

Bram finally relinquished her mouth, his lips

roaming along the curve of her cheekbone to her ear. "Our bodies fit together like pieces of a puzzle." His hand strayed unhindered down her stomach until his fingers encountered the elastic band of her briefs. "We could become wonderful interlocking pieces. I like that idea." His teeth nipped the sensitive area below her earlobe. "In fact, I'd like to just interlock with you for the rest of my life."

Reason scared off Roxanne's passion. "What . . . what did you say?"

"What I'm trying to say"—Bram moved to cradle her head between his hands—"is that I've fallen in love with you."

"You . . . you're crazy."

"No, I'm quite positive. I love you." He enunciated each word with care. "I like the sound of that."

She found herself groping for a sane anchor. "Listen, Abraham Tyler, you just don't fall in love with someone in thirty-six hours."

He considered that for a moment. "You don't believe in love at first sight?"

"No."

"How long should it take to fall in love?"

"Well, for heaven's sake, what a question!" Roxanne pushed him off her and sat up, quickly pulling the front of her shirt together.

Bram rested his chin on her shoulder. "Do you have an answer?"

"No."

"But you know you're not in love with me?"

Her teeth sank into her lower lip. "Look, if you're perfectly honest with yourself, you'll admit you're not in love with me either." She shrugged her shoulder free and turned toward him. "You are a victim of circumstance. You're trapped here when you really want to be lounging on a sandy white beach surrounded by the blue Caribbean. It's . . . it's subliminal seduction. You've mentally exchanged one romantic encounter with another that's convenient."

He scratched his chin. "So you think that I think you're just a convenience."

"Right . . . right," Roxanne nodded eagerly. "If you can't love the one you want, love the one you're with."

"That's one of the best ardor-dampeners I've ever heard. Aunt Mathilda again."

Roxanne almost sputtered something quite profane but restrained herself. "Actually I thought it was psychologically profound."

"Hmmm, I'll have to sleep on that."

"What a good idea." She nudged him back onto his own pillows. "I'm sure by the time morning comes, you'll see that this was just a case of temporary insanity."

Bram yawned. "Who knows"—he kept his tone light—"you could be right," he yawned again and pulled the coverlet around his shoulders.

She punched a pillow into softness before her head landed on it. *Of course I'm right,* Roxanne silently declared. *You don't fall in love in two days. It's just not possible. Even if it was, even if I did, I would fight against it. I don't need to fall in love with any man—especially Bram Tyler.*

Her arm made a protective barrier across her chest

but her traitorous body still savored the pleasure of Bram's touch. The more Roxanne tried to erase the memory of that encounter, the more vivid it became. His inherent masculine scent teased her as did the caresses and kisses from his phantom mouth and hands. Her body responded in kind and began to ache for fullfillment. Her lips twisted in self-deprecation. It was going to be a very long night.

CHAPTER SIX

Roxanne woke on Sunday morning with a giant chip on her shoulder. A chip that steadily grew to mountainous proportions as she listened to the newscaster's glib weather report ". . . forty-five inches of snow, winds gusting to fifty miles per hour, drifts thirty to forty feet, with an ice storm on the way." An extremely good-humored Abraham Tyler only aggravated her more, bringing her breakfast in bed.

She didn't like the way he was watching her or his disgustingly solicitous manner. She also found his smile, his big blue eyes, his handsome, freshly shaven face and his stalwart, athletic physique enormously irritating. After all, hadn't she spent the better part of the night dreaming and fantasizing about those same damnably desirable attributes!

Bram waited until Roxanne had downed a second cup of coffee before he spoke a single word. "Good morning, looks as though we'll be spending New Year's Eve as guests of the Hepworth Hilton."

"New Year's! Tonight's New Year's Eve? Great!"

The coffee container became mangled by her angry fingers. "Just great!" Roxanne tossed the crumbled plastic into the wastebasket near the desk and glared at it when it missed the target.

"Did you have other plans?" Bram's mouth formed an exaggerated grimace as she transferred her evil-eyed stare to him. "Woke up on the wrong side of the bed, did we?" His face was lightened by a happy smile. "Well, I did give you the opportunity to wake up on *my* side."

"Don't start that again!" Roxanne warned, scrambling to her feet. "I'm not fool enough to believe that calling sex *making love* leads to a loving relationship."

"Another selected passage from the teachings of Aunt Mathilda."

Roxanne raised an imperative hand, turned it into a clenched fist, issued a guttural muttering, and stalked past his grinning face to seek the sober confines of the ladies' room.

Her tongue wagged at her reflection. "Why are you wasting all this perfectly good anger on that man?" Roxanne asked herself while carefully peeling away the bandage on her scalp.

Because he's worth the anger. Worth the anxiety. Worth the inner turmoil.

"Two against one, huh!" Brown eyes sent a glittering threat to their mirrored twins. "You're in for a surprise! I'm stronger than both of you put together."

Pronouncing her contusion and her senses healed, Roxanne further investigated the contents of Bram's

111

travel kit. The problem with using his toiletries, she discovered, was the fact that she smelled just like him. The musky scent wrapped her body in invisible arms that held her prisoner.

On the bottom of his bag, she discovered a sample packet of shampoo autographed by Pierre Cardin. Roxanne ripped across the dotted line and released the compelling fragrance. Pierre may have created, she acknowledged, but when Abraham Tyler wore it, it was he who gave it the *coup de foudre*—the bolt of lightning—that kept demolishing her willpower and undermining her reason.

"Damn the man!" Quickly Roxanne leaned under the faucet, soaked her head with ice cold water, and wished it were possible to wash him out of her hair as easily as she washed his essence in.

The shampoo and a hot, soapy sponge bath put her in a better frame of mind, as did using a little blusher and lipstick. By the time the wall-mounted air blower finished doing double-duty as a hair and clothes dryer, Roxanne felt crisp, confident, in control, and ready to tangle with anything or anyone.

Bram's humming turned into a wolf whistle when she walked into the lounge. "You are amazing," he announced in a tone of profound respect. "Each morning you've managed to look neat, fresh, and elegant despite the lack of suitable amenities."

"Why, thank you." Her hand ruffled freshly washed curls as she gave a regal nod. "You do remarkably well yourself," came her truthful compliment. "I don't suppose a miracle has occurred and there's been a change in the weather?"

He shook his head. "Not according to the ten o'clock news. If you look out the window, you'll see ice as thick as my arm coating the flagpole—that is when the wind lets up so you can see the flagpole."

"It's those damn volcanoes and the satellites NASA sends into outer space," Roxanne grumbled. "They keep tampering with Mother Nature and she doesn't like it." She slid a quarter off the table and went to the vending machine. The Empty light flashed on when she pressed for an apple. She selected an orange and listened to the coin instead of the fruit tumble into the bin. "We've exhausted this machine," Roxanne reported.

Bram turned in his chair. "I was surprised it kept delivering as long as it did. Since the lounge was opened in September, the fruit and yogurt machine has been the most popular. The sandwiches and candy should still be stocked. The staff has been eating their lunches standing in long Christmas return and exchange lines rather than here."

Her eyes scanned the pleasant surroundings. "This is a nice idea."

"Bankers are nice people." He found pleasure in her responding smile. "How about reopening the Hepworth Casino?" Bram tapped the deck. "All the cards have been thoroughly shuffled."

"Shuffled or stacked?" Roxanne parried, settling in her chair.

He exhaled a long, theatrical sigh. "Thank God, you're back to your normal witty self."

For the rest of the morning until mid-afternoon Bram purposefully kept the conversation light and

113

inconsequential, hoping to further relax Roxanne. At least that was his intention until he kept steadily losing. "Say, you're not cheating, are you?"

Roxanne made a production of rolling up the long sleeves on his shirt. "Nothing up them."

"How much am I into you for now?"

She sucked in her cheeks and totaled the score. "You *owe* me one thousand eight hundred thirty-five dollars and forty cents."

"I prefer *into.*"

"So you said last night."

His dark brows rose in appreciation. "Touché. Is that why I heard your lovely rendition of "Ain't Misbehavin' " this morning?"

"Touché yourself," came her easy retort. "It's your deal."

"I've been thinking a lot about last night."

"I thought you'd get around to it."

He stopped shuffling the flower-decorated cards and looked at his watch. "We've been together a total of forty-seven hours. Considering the usual date lasts on average four hours, and you have, say, three dates a week, this is our twelfth date and our fourth week together." His blue eyes focused on her face. "Is that a more appropriate length of time for me to say I love you?"

Roxanne rolled her eyes. "You're only saying what you think I want to hear."

"And you don't want to hear that?"

"I don't believe it." The chip had returned to her shoulder. "Look, I'm not interested in racking up sack time with you. If you wanted to end this year with a bang, you've marooned yourself with the wrong woman." Roxanne sucked air through her clenched teeth. "Damn you, Bram, stop laughing!"

"I just find it very amusing the way you're able to sabotage your own feelings about me." He placed the shuffled cards before her.

"I don't have any feelings about you to sabotage!" Roxanne hissed, cutting the cards with surprising viciousness.

Bram stroked his jaw. "Really? As I recall, last night . . ." His smile broadened into a grin. "Now, now, Roxanne, you didn't growl like that last night." He benignly ignored her brown eyes that narrowed into dangerous slits. "You purred when I kissed you, and you kissed me back quite passionately."

He began tossing cards at her. "And your hands . . . mmm . . . they were managing to hold me tight and even stroked my back. Those nonsensitive nipples of yours responded rather excitedly to my—"

"Do you mind!"

"I love it when you blush." He flipped over the first discard and proceeded to look at his hand.

She blinked rapidly, trying to focus on her cards. "I—I've read articles about men like you. Men who are unusually romantic; men who create fantasies about the women they meet and weave all sorts of wild scenarios in their mind."

"Oh, I'll admit to the fantasies—especially in regards to you," he asserted. "But to be perfectly honest, Roxanne, I'm no Lothario. I'm not out to set a Guinness record for using women. I respect the female sex. But I know what I want, and I've finally

115

found it in you." Bram looked over the tops of his cards, his expression totally serious. "Believe me, I was very surprised about the intensity of my feelings. Initially I thought it was just a case of adolescent infatuation. Now I realize I was just denying the truth."

"What is your version of the truth?"

"That it is possible to know someone for so short a time and feel that everything is so right."

Roxanne was growing impatient. "You've decided that I'm your Miss Right?"

He nodded. "I know you well enough to—"

"You *think* you know me," she interrupted, "but you don't."

"Really?" Bram considered her statement for a moment. "You mean your reaction last night was not unusual? That you readily melt against just *any* man? Come alive like that when just *any* man holds you and touches you? Make those adorable little mewing sounds when just *any* man kisses and caresses your gorgeous body?"

"No, I do not!" Viewing his grinning face, she hastily corrected herself. "You misunderstood my point."

"That is the point," he countered. "I did not misunderstand. I understand you all too well and your reaction to me is directly related to the brain-washing by your aunt."

Roxanne suppressed the urge to scream. Instead, she drew a card. "This is the eminent psychiatrist talking now, is it?"

"Aunt Mathilda is a formidable obstacle to overcome, but I'm just the man to do it." He swooped up her discard. "I told you this before, but I don't mind repeating it. I love you. I intend to make love to you before the New Year dawns."

"That sounds more like a threat than an endearment," she pointed out ruthlessly. "Is that the Tyler method? Threatening women into submission."

"Women usually threaten me into submission," Bram chided her. "You just don't realize what a wonderful man you've lucked into. But you will."

"I love me, whom do you love?" came her sarcastic jeer.

"I love you," he returned easily, again claiming another discarded club. "Considering the fact Mathilda had you under her concrete thumb for—what was it?—seven or eight years, you turned out pretty well."

Roxanne had to laugh. "Gee, thanks."

"I'm serious."

"I know you are." She struggled to swallow another laugh.

"It couldn't have been easy being a nurse-companion to a crabby spinster, puckered on both ends, who was soured on love and cursed life in general."

Her eyes widened. "Is that your considered opinion of Aunt Mathilda?"

Bram's dark head made a modest bow. "Spare me the compliments. I pegged the old biddy perfectly, didn't I?" Without waiting for Roxanne to agree, he continued. "Mathilda's specter haunts you. You're afraid to let yourself go, let yourself feel, let yourself love."

117

"Whom do you want me to go, feel, and love?" she inquired, tossing out another club.

"Me of course." His blue gaze leveled a peremptory gaze. "Only me. Tut, tut, you're getting careless." He reached for the card. "I realize it's going to take constant tutelage on my part to exorcise Mathilda's fiendish control."

"That's so wonderful of you. So selfless and generous." Roxanne took his discarded spade and deftly laid down a perfect rummy meld. "Gin."

Bram muttered an expletive. "I know what the problem is. I know why I'm losing."

She added another mountain of points to her score before reassembling the cards. "What's your excuse this time?" Roxanne shuffled, waited for Bram to cut and began to deal.

"Not enough incentive."

"I'm perfectly willing to raise the limit to a dollar a point. You've already funded my IRA for next year; I can let you start on my Keogh."

"Money was not the incentive I was talking about." He smiled with approval at his hand and began to adjust his cards according to suits.

Roxanne stared at him with growing suspicion. "What *is* your idea of the right incentive?"

"Strip gin would be interesting." He drew the first card. "Of course, I know what your reaction would be and I can hear Aunt Mathilda shrieking in horror, a lace hanky pressed to her mouth while she hunts for the smelling salts to ward off the vapors."

"Aunt Mathilda, vapors? Hmmm. Strip gin?" Roxanne picked a card and slowly began to organize her hand. "I really think it's time I told you the truth about me and my family and, especially, Aunt Mathilda." Roxanne tutted Bram silent when he tried to interrupt.

"Mathilda was born in New York City at the turn of the century. In 1922 she got her first job. Ever hear of Minsky's?" She fluttered her lashes and smiled. "Take ten terrific girls and only nine costumes? Aunt Mathilda was the *tenth* girl.

"She'd adore playing strip gin, especially if she could lose. And with all due respect to your *minor* in psychiatry, I have no inhibitions at playing either." One at a time Roxanne displayed her cards on the table. "Gin." Her fingers folded together, her expression guileless. "I'll take your shirt."

Bram struggled to talk around a tongue that swelled like a sponge. "This is . . . you are . . . you're joking. Right?"

"About gin, Auntie, or taking your shirt?" Roxanne shook her head. "Say"—her eyes narrowed—"not welching on the bet, are you?"

His muttered curses were drowned under a sea of terry cloth as he pulled the tennis shirt over his head. "So the Victorian Aunt never existed. Mathilda was, as H. L. Mencken coined, an ecdysiast, and you've been secretly laughing at me all this time!" Bram tossed the shirt at her. His eyes echoed his hair—black with a burnishment of cobalt blue. "What else have you been laughing at, fair Roxanne?"

"I wasn't exactly laughing at you," she protested, her tone decidedly censorial. "I wanted to prove to you that even after twelve dates and four weeks you've yet to really know the woman you claim to love." Roxanne found her smugness and complacent attitude dissipating under an onslaught of pure feminine awareness and appreciation of Abraham Tyler's naked torso.

She could easily list a dozen women who'd swoon over viewing a chest like his—including Aunt Mathilda! *Especially Aunt Mathilda,* her mind teased her. *She was a lady who reveled in viewing an undraped body, artistic adoration notwithstanding.*

Bram's upper body would inspire any artist to take pastels in hand to capture on paper his magnificent male form. Roxanne's half-hooded eyes flowed along the sinewy landscape of his broad shoulders before transversing a voyeur's path through the curly black hair that forested his firm flesh.

She silently cursed the sport of tennis for contributing to Bram's athletic physique. Why couldn't his chest have been concave and in dire need of Nautilus training? Why hadn't she asked for his pants!

Pants! Roxanne inhaled a squeak. "Wake up!" She pushed the cards at him. "It's your deal, for heaven's sake!" Ignoring his raised eyebrow, she began to fold the terry shirt that dangled half off the table.

"So tell me, Roxanne, where else did I go wrong?" Bram's able fingers shuffled the cards thoroughly. "How about your aunt's house? No horsehair sofa, no heavy velvet drapes, no doilies, no fans?"

"You were right about the architecture. It is a prewar bungalow," she reported. Her fingertips kept smoothing his discarded shirt, savoring the warmth from his body that clung to the material.

Roxanne cleared her throat. "The furnishings are stylishly traditional with a few antiques here and there. No velvet or doilies, but we do have fans." Dark lashes lowered demurely. "Two giant pastel pink ostrich plumes that form a design over the headboard of Aunt Mathilda's waterbed." Her laughter undermined his low groan.

"Waterbed!"

"Purely medicinal. Mathilda had arthritis." Suddenly Roxanne lost her teasing attitude. "What a cruel disease." Her pensive eyes locked onto Bram's face. "I wish you could have known Aunt in her heyday. She was a delightful mix of Isadora Duncan, Mae West, and Auntie Mame. A true terpsichorean tease. She was burlesque even after it folded.

"At eighty Mathilda still had a young, vibrant, witty mind and soul that was a prisoner in a crippled body. It was my pleasure to move in and take care of her when she had her hip replaced. I helped her through all forms of therapy, watched helplessly as she deteriorated even after taking gold shots. I have never been so frustrated. Nothing worked." Her fist hit the table. "Nothing. The damn disease completely crippled her and finally took its toll on her heart."

Roxanne watched as her white-knuckled fist was consumed by a large, comforting hand. Bram's voice was equally soothing when he spoke. "You were there for her; you were her strength. I wish I'd have known you then; I could have been there for you." His fingers pried hers open, his thumb made caress-

121

ing gestures in her palm. "My grandfather outlived my own parents and, as I watched him pass out of my life, I remember thinking I'm the loser and the lost. I comforted him, but who can comfort me."

She nodded in empathy. "The loser and the lost. It's funny, really, I was lost before that. Mathilda helped me find myself. In many respects she made me believe in myself."

"A mentor?"

"A supporter. A sounding board. A clear thinker when I was dealing with a clouded brain."

Bram laughed and shook his head. "I can't imagine you with a clouded brain." He went back to shuffling the cards, then looked at her curiously. "What was his name?"

"Richard Beck." Roxanne's hand clamped over her mouth the instant his name reached her ears. *How could I have said that! Relax, play it cool, and change the subject.* "Are you going to fiddle with those cards forever?" she demanded.

"How nicely you did that." He put the deck in front of her.

"Did what?" She cut.

"Changed the subject."

He reads minds! Roxanne's lips twisted in self-derision. "The subject should have never been brought up. Am I bringing up your past?"

"No, but you can," Bram offered, dealing out the cards. "We could start with Jennifer Lambert." His voice dropped to a conspiratorial whisper. "She was the first. I was twelve, it was summer, and we were behind the Little League scoreboard. . . ."

"How appropriate," came her dry quip.

He gave her his best leer. "I'm just trying to live up to your image."

"Well, don't," Roxanne sassed back. "It doesn't work. You can't be something you're not."

"If anything, I've convinced you I'm not."

She sighed and fanned open her cards. "Same stakes?"

"I'm game." His eyebrows wiggled up and down. "So, tell me about Richard Beck. I don't want to make his mistakes. Forewarned is forearmed."

"Richard didn't make the mistake. I did," Roxanne said after a long moment. "I tried to be Polly Perfect. Fortunately, before it became a marital mistake, I realized I was more like Popeye: I am what I am."

"And Richard didn't like what you am?"

"No, he did not. He liked what I appeared to be." She picked a card, frowned, and tossed it away. "Richard nearly had a coronary when I told him I was starting Greetings. The more I became me, the more little coronaries Richard started having."

"So then it was bye-bye Richard."

"A mutual parting of the engaged couple."

"It had gone that far?"

"Yes . . . that far."

Bram took the discards. "What was Mathilda's impression?"

Roxanne giggled. "She never liked Richard. Too stuffy. Too rigid. Too too! Of course, she had the same problem with men in her line of work. It's hard to find a man who wants to bring a stripper home to

123

meet his mother. Actually"—she was thoughtful for a moment—"I don't think my own mother would have ever married if she hadn't found my dad."

He stuttered in astonishment. "Are . . . are you telling me *your* mother was a stripper too?"

Just to be perverse, Roxanne wanted to say yes. "My mother happens to own two of the seventy-two most beautiful legs in the world." At Bram's bewildered expression, she clarified her statement. "Mother was a Rockette at Radio City Music Hall and then went on to dance in numerous Broadway productions. My father was a choreographer and they met and fell in love while they were doing a show at the Roxy."

"Hence, Roxanne."

She smiled and nodded.

"The roar of the crowd and the smell of the greasepaint is running rampant through your veins," Bram commented, reaching again for the growing discard pack. "Greetings and Saluations was the perfect career choice, unless—did you have Broadway aspirations yourself?"

"Too disciplined an environment. I was never one for routine and constant workouts and time schedules. I even rebelled at going to summer camp." Roxanne's mouth curved in a reminiscent smile. "Aunt Mathilda once said I'd make a great stripper, but they just don't have the class today as they did in the Roaring Twenties. Where have all the Sally Rands and Gypsy Rose Lees gone?"

"They're not in Minneapolis," he agreed. "So

Richard Beck couldn't hack bringing a belly-gram home to Mother?"

Why did he have to bring up Richard again? "A belly-gram, a gorilla-gram, an any-gram. Terribly undignified." Her brown eyes were accusing. "But that's not an unusual reaction. Most men who have distinguished business positions would cringe at having a gorilla-costumed wife. What does Mrs. Hepworth National Bank do for a living?"

Bram thought about that for a moment. "Hmmm. As I recall, she was a private-duty nurse."

"Ahhh . . . Florence Nightingale." Roxanne's smile was tight. "Now, that's dignified."

"I find dignity is in the eye of the beholder."

"Really." She drew another card. "What was the last undignified thing you've done, Abraham Tyler?"

"Sixteen of us jammed into a VW bug for a yearbook picture in college."

"Nothing recent? No walking barefoot during a summer rainstorm? No making angels in the snow? No water fights while washing the car?"

"Nope." He looked down at himself. "How about losing my shirt at cards?" came his fervent inquiry.

"Not all *that* undignified, but why don't we add your shoes too." Roxanne placed her hand face-up on the table. "Gin."

The ensuing silence was punctuated by the thud of shoes landing on the tile floor. "Nothing like being stranded with a card shark," Bram said at last. "This is not the way I had envisioned the game to progress."

"I know." She swept the cards into a pile for her

deal. "There is a certain perverse satisfaction in beating the pants off a banker."

"Shuffle and deal," came his growling directive. By the end of the round Bram had lost his socks. "Let's try a hand of poker, shall we?"

Roxanne protested. "Who said anything about changing the game?"

"Dealer's choice," he returned. "Very simple, five-card draw."

Moments later she was inspecting her hand. "Can you just refresh my memory as to what beats what?"

"A pair, two pair, three of a kind, a straight, flush, full house—"

"You can stop there," Roxanne ordered.

"You're bluffing."

She smiled. "I'll play these."

He called her bluff and lost his watch.

"I think I like poker. Let's try seven-card stud, low card in the hole is wild."

Bram hissed. "You hustler. So Auntie taught you poker too."

"I did tell you I had a social education," Roxanne reminded him sweetly and flipped a card across the table. "Let's make this the last hand. I'm hungry and tired of sitting. Maybe I'll jog around the fourth floor."

"Last hand." He inspected his cards. "How about double or nothing?"

Roxanne laughed. "Double or nothing? You're down to your pants and your B.V.D.'s, buster."

"I'd be interested in seeing what you'd do with a naked man," came his easy rejoinder. "Of course, it would also be interesting to see what would happen if I should win."

"You win?" She looked at the two cards she was holding, and grinned. "What did you say beats what?"

"Oh, no," Bram warned, "you're not going to psych me out with that gag again." He fingered through the four cards that were face up in front of her. "I can't see that you have anything exciting here."

She viewed his cards. "The feeling is mutual. Of course everything changes with the seventh card." Roxanne picked up the deck and dealt the finale facedown. With enigmatic intensity she selected the most powerful five cards and formed her winning hand. "Read 'em and weep—full house: fives and sevens."

Blue eyes sparkled in delightful triumph. "Not this time, baby. Four three's." Bram leaned over and chucked her under the chin. "Victory, how sweet it is! Oh, grin and *bare* it, Roxy." He winked and leaned back in the chair. "Now, what two items of clothing should I choose?"

I feel like a prize mare at auction! Roxanne watched Bram rise from the chair to stand and tower over her. *Helpless.* She swallowed hard. *Helpless and . . . and . . .* Roxanne swallowed again as helplessness crossed the boundary line and stirred hidden feelings that lurked in a secret section of her soul.

An oddly sweet tightening of her muscles sent little prickles of desire percolating through her veins. Her eyes performed a double duty: visually caressing his naked muscular chest and slim hard-bellied torso while her fingers tingled under the memory of actually touching his warm hair-rough flesh last night.

Suddenly Roxanne wanted to share this moment —share herself with him. She saw his chest rise and fall with increasing intensity in unison with her own. Still seated, she began to tremble under the all-encompassing need to have Bram make his decision. She wore only four items of clothing: his shirt, her panties, and his tennis socks. Impatient for his verdict and anxious to appease her own hunger, Roxanne's hand moved to the top button on the shirt.

"I'll take your socks."

"My . . . my socks?" Her fingers splayed across the hollow of her throat, her voice crackling in disappointment.

Crouching on the floor, Bram took in Roxanne's flushed face and flustered demeanor and favored her with a lazy smile. "Just thinking about the unexplored erogenous zones at the back of your knees is driving me insane."

His hands cupped her right foot; his pinkies scrolled slowly along her sensitive sole while his thumbs delineated every toe through the thick white socks. "You have your mother's legs, dancer's legs," he proclaimed, "sleek, elegant, seemingly never-ending.

"Slender calves but strong"—his fingers lightly pressed into her muscles—"smooth knees and firm thighs." Bram's husky voice betrayed his fervent emotions.

Roxanne mentally tried to calm a heart that

pounded in the most absurd rhythm. *The man is only removing a sock,* she rudely reminded herself. *Only a sock!* She concentrated on that thought while she focused on that object.

Virile masculine fingers took infinite time in peeling down the blue-banded white cotton hose. She watched his fingers and palms encircle her leg. Her skin flushed under the warm caress of his hands. A pleasurable sigh emanated from her throat and Roxanne had to grip the seat of her chair to stop herself from touching the midnight silk that was Bram's hair.

Abruptly the lights went out, plunging the lounge into darkness. "Oh, hell!" Bram swore. "Just when I was getting to the good part!"

CHAPTER SEVEN

Roxanne's eyes blinked rapidly, trying to adjust to the sudden loss of light. She stared at the ceiling. "I don't suppose it's just a burnt-out fluorescent?"

"Try no power."

"That's what I thought you'd say. Maybe it will come right back on." Her tone was hopeful.

Bram sat on the edge of the table and cocked his head. "Listen to that wind. Old Man Winter and Mother Nature have been battling and we were so involved in our card game that we failed to notice."

"Does the bank have a back-up generator?"

"A battery alarm system takes over in the vault," he explained, "but if you're wondering about the heat and lights . . ."

Roxanne shuddered. "I get the picture. Hot cash; frozen people."

Leaning forward, his hands cupped her face and his voice teased her. "Don't worry, honey, I can think of all sorts of ways to warm your assets."

"Oh, you bankers, always ready to make a deposit," she cooed, then gave a yelp as she was yanked against his frame and held prisoner by his arms.

"Shared bodily warmth." Bram's face nuzzled the side of her neck, his splayed hands possessively mapping her tapered back. "Hmmm . . . Roxy, you feel wonderful. We fit together perfectly."

Roxanne let her arms hang limply at her side and refused to acknowledge that his mouth was settling butterfly kisses just beneath her right ear. Ten minutes ago she had craved this very scenario and now that it was happening, she needed to stop it.

Needed? Yes. When she had time to think about loving Abraham Tyler she became indecisive. One minute hot, the next cold. What was happening to her? A nice, dependable, sensible woman like her should not be caught in a feverish, unexpected, disconcerting situation like this! "Do . . . do you have a match?"

Bram squeezed her waist and kissed her chin. "You don't need a match to light my fire."

Roxanne hastily dodged his seeking lips. "I need a match to light the candles so we don't curse the darkness," she replied in a tone of patient forbearance.

He straightened. "Now look who's acting stuffy and dignified," Bram complained, reluctantly abandoning her body to search through his pants pockets. "No matches, but here's my penlight." A click sounded and a tiny beam lanced across Roxanne's face. "I was trying to act more like you, and you go and turn responsible and mature."

She patted his cheek. "Someone has to be. I'll hunt

131

for matches while you get dressed." Roxanne moved around him and began to pull out drawers. Her "Eureka" sounded, and quickly the wicks on the three Santa candles caught fire and filled the lounge in flickering amber shadows. "There, isn't that much better?" She placed the tiny flashlight back on the table.

Bram looked up from pulling on his socks. "No. I enjoyed playing with you in the dark."

Roxanne's brow arched at his tone. "I didn't know vice presidents whined."

He flicked on the penlight, held it under his chin, made a face at her, and snapped it off. *Talk about extended adolescence!* Bram silently chided himself. *Every time I advance, the lady retreats. I could feel the armor plating her body, shielding her from a natural response. And I wasn't fooling myself about the response; it was there.*

Moody blue eyes watched as Roxanne tidied the room and grouped the flaming Santas into one vivid candelabrum. Bram grew thoughtful. *Maybe a change in strategy is warranted. I don't like playing games but*—a smile curved his lips—*if it's possible, I'd like to make a mountain move!*

Arms crossed, he made himself comfortable in the chair and cultivated a bored and somewhat melancholy attitude. "Well, what's next?"

"Dinner." Her tongue clicked against the roof of her mouth at hearing his groan. "Honestly, Bram, you'd think you had to go out into the frozen tundra and kill a polar bear." Roxanne walked over to him.

"How hard is it to drop a few quarters into a machine?"

"Very—when the machine runs on electricity and there is none," he pointed out succinctly. "You know, I can't help thinking if I had just left for the airport an hour earlier maybe I could have boarded another flight and right now . . ." A pleasurable sigh escaped him. "I'd be lying on the beach, sipping a piña colada and watching all the bikinis go by."

His statement struck Roxanne a powerful blow. Hadn't he been the one talking about fate throwing them together and, even though it had been quick, how much he loved her. Now . . . now the man had the gall to say he would easily trade her for sand, a drink, and another woman! She hissed. "What nerve!"

"Did you say something?"

"Yes!" Roxanne snapped and drew a deep breath. "If *I* had left right after delivering your belly-gram, I would be in my own house, wrapped in my fluffy blue robe, reading in front of a roaring fire!"

Her hands clamped around his wrists, her voice increasing in anger. "And since neither of us can be anyplace else, we are going to have our own New Year's Eve party, complete with a candlelight dinner just as soon as you"—she cleared her throat, regained her composure, and yanked him from the chair—"as soon as you figure out how to break into the vending machines."

Bram choked down a laugh. "From banker to burglar." He pretended to ponder that observation a moment. "You know, it's amazing how fast my dignity flees when I'm with you."

"What a cheap crack! Who's the one who wanted to play strip gin?" came her sarcastic reminder.

"Maybe it was the company I was keeping." He walked around her to the cabinets and aimed the tiny flashlight inside one after another. "Maybe Aunt Mathilda's spirit has taken possession of—"

"Will you please just look for something to open the lock with," Roxanne ordered, tugging open a drawer. "What's in here?"

The beam peaked inside. "Plastic forks, knives, and spoons." He pushed it closed and opened another. "Aha! A nail file and—whoops, look at this." Bram held up a small plastic case with three screwdrivers inside. "Our dinner ticket. Follow me, accomplice in crime. You can hold the light."

Roxanne focused the penlight on the vending machine lock. "What do you think? Piece of cake?"

He withdrew a small Phillips-head screwdriver, eased it into the center of the mechanism, and wiggled it back and forth. Nothing happened. "I think I should watch more crime shows on TV." Bram applied more muscle while fervently praying to hear the magic *click*.

"How about using this flat one to pry it open?" she suggested, the light bouncing as she juggled the tool. "I can get a bobby pin from my purse, or how about a credit card? I once popped the lock on my front door with my MasterCard."

Bram wrenched out the screwdriver and looked at her. "Remind me to double-check the vault before

134

you leave," he remarked dryly, taking the proffered tool. "I had no idea your talents also extended to burglary." Sliding the wedge-shaped screwdriver between the lock and the door unit, Bram used his fist like a hammer, pounding in the handle and then pushing the steel blade upward. He was rewarded by a metallic groan and the liberation of the sandwich machine. *"Voilà!"*

She squeezed his bicep. "Bravo! Speaking of talent"—Roxanne nodded toward the soft drink machine—"you can use yours on that while I select dinner. We should eat all the mayonnaise dressing first."

"No matter how I try, I can't make this tuna taste like lobster." Bram toasted the last half of his sandwich over the candle flame. "You know, they serve five-pound lobsters on St. Croix and all sorts of exotic libations in pineapple and coconut shells."

"What a shame you have to settle for tuna, milk, and little old me," Roxanne sneered, irritation prickling her body. She stood up. "Do you want a Mounds bar?"

He grinned at her tone and rubbed his face. "No, thanks, I think I'll jog around the fourth floor." Bram scraped his chair back. "I'll pretend I'm running on the beach, the tropical breeze blowing through the palm trees, a schooner silhouetted on the bay by the coral sunset."

Under the safety of the shadows Roxanne stuck her tongue out at him. "I'll just tidy up." She hoped she sounded oblivious and carefree.

135

"You do *that* so well," came his cheery comment as he loped out the door.

"'You do that so well,'" she mimicked, her tongue stabbing the air again. Perversely Roxanne yanked another candy bar free of the machine and resettled herself at the table.

Her fingers zigzagged over the fat-bellied candle Santas and chipped at the dribbled trail of red wax. "I did try to create a party mood," Roxanne muttered around bites of dark chocolate and sweet coconut. She sighed and looked up, expecting Bram to jog past.

"It's not as though I miss the man." Her thumbnail scratched away a paraffin puddle that plopped onto the table. "Three days ago I didn't even know Abraham Tyler existed. How could I miss him? He just left the room. He can't leave the building. He'll be back any minute." Again brown eyes took up the vigil of staring at the door.

"This is stupid." Roxanne pushed free of the chair. "I am acting stupid and all because of *him!*" She busied her idle hands with picking up the garbage and cleaning the table.

Rereading all the magazines by candlelight occupied her for a while although her eyes and ears were busy listening for her supposedly jogging companion. Frustrated, annoyed and uncomfortably confused about her feelings, Roxanne angrily tossed *Newsweek* across the room.

"Damn that man!" Her balled fist smacked her palm. "It's not fair. There's no way you can fall in love with someone in fifty-six hours. Not even if it equals twelve dates, well, fourteen after lunch and dinner, and four weeks and . . ."

Her fingers rudely agitated her curls. "He's driven me insane. People who talk to themselves are certifiable. I can think of a hundred reasons to hate Bram Tyler." Her lips twisted in a smirk. "But I'm not going to. I'm not going to think about him at all."

Roxanne noticed that the wall clock had ceased marking time at eight twelve, but that was many hours ago. "It must be close to midnight," she mused. "The crowds filling Times Square would be waiting to count the old year down into a new one." The battery pack in the recorder was new, and she reasoned that one local station would be broadcasting New Year's Eve in Manhattan even if New Year's Eve in Minneapolis was snowbound, below zero, and both power- and partyless.

"I will ring in Baby New Year all by my lonesome," she announced on a positive note, and yanked a bag of corn chips from the vending machine. "Lonesome? I am not lonesome," Roxanne corrected herself. She put one candle in an ashtray and blew out the others. "I am thoroughly enjoying my solitary state." With that, she left the lounge and headed for Bram's office.

If the music was any indication, WCCO was ushering out the 1940s. Roxanne wiggled herself into a comfortable position on the padded window seat, munched the corn chips, and doodled on the frosted glass while she listed to Glenn Miller's clarinet blend with saxophones to play "Moonlight Serenade."

She tried not to think about Bram and ended up

trying to think about what he must be thinking. Maybe it was her background. Perhaps hearing about Aunt Mathilda and her parents coupled with her own very theatrical, out-of-the-ordinary business had given him cause to rethink those hastily issued words of love.

"Fickle!" Roxanne's teeth sank a vicious bite into a chip that sent the back end scattering over her shirt. "He's just like Richard—concerned with propriety!" Exhaling a heavy sigh, she found herself rationalizing on Bram's behalf. "Bram isn't anything like Richard, and, to be fair, especially with his new position, I'd imagine he would have to be dignified and above reproach."

Some long-forgotten vocalist was singing "Outside of That I Love You," making Roxanne more moody than before, and just as Frank Sinatra started crooning "This Love of Mine" the object of her thoughts walked in the door. "How many miles down the beach did you do?"

Bleakness tempered her sarcastic retort and Bram found that telltale emotion thrilled him. "Relocated the party in here?" His hip edged her feet to one side as he settled on the brown leather cushion. "Will they be switching to Times Square in eight minutes?"

Roxanne gave an unconcerned shrug. "I suppose." She extended the bag of chips. "Sorry it's not St. Croix-ish. What do they snack on in the islands?"

"Not these." The candle flame bathed her in a tawny sunset glow and Bram was having a hard time disguising the pleasure he was feeling just being near her. His right hand circled her wrist; his left plucked the plastic bag free and tossed it on the desk. "They do dance in the islands."

She wasn't quite sure how it happened, but in one fluid movement Roxanne found herself on her feet, in his arms, and swaying to "As Time Goes By."

Bram forced himself not to look at her; instead, he focused on the busy candle flame that came into view over her left shoulder. "You're a wonderful dancer."

He is so remote! Roxanne gnawed her lower lip. *He's holding me the way the boys in the fifth grade hold a girl when they first learn the box step.* "Does . . . does my being from a long line of dancers of one type or another bother you?" she finally garnered the nerve to ask.

"Nope, not one bit."

Roxanne wiggled her right hand out of his left, moved it to his shoulder, then slid both her hands along his collarbone. She became preoccupied with him. Her fingers stealthily crept around his neck to filter through the thick black waves that sculpted his head.

Her body closed the gap between them, her thighs, hips, and breasts snug against his athletic contours. Roxanne wasn't quite sure of the rhyme or reason of it but decided not to think and just feel. Her usual rationale had been swept away by dark blue eyes, lean features, an easy smile, and a superbly masculine, but definitely not Cyrano-ish, nose.

Despite her maneuvers, the masculine hands that rested on her hips were as impersonal as Bram's still-stoic features. Roxanne hissed at his lack of reaction.

"Did you say something?"

"No." The word was clipped and high. Sighing, she swallowed her inhibitions and cleared her throat, but the radio announcer's voice surpassed hers.

"We're switching to Times Square for the last ten seconds of the year. Nine . . . eight . . . seven . . . six . . . five. The golden ball is falling. Three . . . two . . . one! Happy New Year!"

"Happy New Year, Roxanne Murdoch."

"Happy New Year, Abraham Tyler." She waited a moment, then frowned. "Don't I even get the traditional Happy New Year kiss?"

"Sure." Bram lifted her chin and placed a quick, light kiss on her lips. "There you are."

Roxanne pouted. "That was a pretty lousy kiss. My brother's guinea pig kisses better than that when you give him a carrot." Her hands clamped on either side of his head, her fingers roughly threading through silver-sketched sideburns. "This . . . is more what I had in mind."

She put everything she had into that kiss. Her lips sealed tightly on his, stealing his breath and making it her own. Her tongue was a teasing invader that delightfully probed inside his mouth and savored the intimacy of tangling with its mate. Suddenly she broke the intimate coupling. "Are—are you still thinking about bikini-clad girls?" Her low voice was shaky.

Bram's gaze held brown eyes that looked soft and vulnerable. "It was very strange about those bikini-clad girls." His arms formed a powerful belt around her waist. "They all were blessed with your face."

His lips pressed quick kisses along her brow bone, her temple, her cheek, till they reached the corner of her mouth. "I love you."

Roxanne's lips spoke against his. "Then why did you leave me?"

"You missed me?" His tongue traced the gentle cupid's bow.

Her head tilted, her tone accusing. "You wanted me to miss you."

"Did I succeed?"

Her arms slid around his neck, her body burrowing tighter. "Yes. I was lonely rather than alone." Roxanne rested her cheek against his shoulder, the warmth of his body penetrating the terry shirt. "That's never happened to me before. I don't quite understand—"

"I'll do the understanding for both of us," Bram said curtly. His hand caught her chin and lifted her face. "I know this defies rational explanation, but at thirty-eight I know myself and what I want. And, Roxanne, I want and need you very much." He fingered a luxurious tendril that curled around her ear. "Every day with you gets better and better. I can't imagine how I ever got through twenty-four hours without knowing you'd be there for me."

She turned and kissed his palm. "Oh, Bram, I . . ."

His mouth silenced her. "You're starting to think again and I'm not going to let you. Do you trust me?"

She nodded.

"Show me."

Her lips were soft and sweet as they reunited with his, her fingers tingling in delightful anticipation as they splayed across his chest and playfully tangled with the dark curls that escaped through the unbuttoned shirt placket. "There is one thing I must think about," Roxanne managed somewhat shyly. "I was wondering how far away your box of Boy Scout virtues is?"

"My desk drawer."

"That's a little too far away." Brown eyes locked with blue. "Do you mind, because I haven't anything and—"

"There's nothing I'd mind where you're concerned." Bram kissed her hard before releasing her to get the tiny foil packet. He snapped off the radio, checked the safety of the candle, and then returned to Roxanne.

She was sitting on the mattress of pillows that littered the carpet, feeling hesitant and nervous, but all that dissolved the instant Bram embraced her.

"You were shaking." He pulled her onto his lap, one arm tightening at her waist while his free hand caressed the curve of her jaw.

"I was wondering if I could compete with Jennifer Lambert and her Little League scoreboard technique."

"You're way ahead of Jennifer," Bram returned solemnly. "She wore an undershirt and had short legs." Effortlessly the buttons on the oxford cloth were released, allowing his hand to conform completely to her full breast. "You feel like silk."

A pleasurable sigh escaped her as the tips of his

fingers drew a series of delicate little circles that hardened her nipple. Her hand crept beneath the terry material the shielded his torso, her palm experiencing the rugged landscape of his body.

Bram kissed her again—taking his time, enjoying the sweet nectar that gave him sustenance. His mouth moved lower, down her throat to the creamy swell of her breast. "God, Roxanne, you're beautiful." A hungry growl formed in his throat as his lips and tongue sampled a rosy peak.

She lifted herself closer, her entire body burning with delight. "Oh, that feels wonderful. . . ." His teeth nipped lightly, making her tremble and cling tighter. "Bram . . ." Her hand pushed his head up so her lips could rain light kisses on his face. "I love your nose."

"Only the nose?" he teased.

"It's the only thing I can get at!" Roxanne tugged at his shirt. "I hadn't realized you were so modest." A giggle bubbled in surprise at her own shocking behavior. What was happening to her? She had never displayed such an urgent appetite. Her gaze wandered over his lean physique, looking for a way to be turned off, only to find her hunger piqued. By way of example, she slipped her shirt off and tossed it on the sofa, following it with her socks.

"Hmmm, and what about this?" His finger snapped the elastic leg band on her apricot panties.

"Oh, I thought you could handle that." Leaning on her elbows, Roxanne watched Bram pull off his shirt and socks and dispose of his pants, leaving a pair of light-blue briefs. "I'm not the only one with great legs." Her hand curved around a hard-muscled calf, fingernails making erotic squiggles against the hair-rough flesh.

On hearing his sigh of approval, her hand and fingers continued their exploring venture along his thigh to his hips. Her palm strayed across the front of his briefs. "You were right"—her voice was a shy whisper—"your cute nose is certainly not indicative of your virility."

"Tell me more," Bram commanded.

She shook her head. "You'll only get a swelled head."

His hands nipped at her waist and pulled her fully onto his chest. "That's not what's swelling." His eyes worshiped her every feature. "You make me feel like a young boy. I could climb Mt. Everest and touch the stars."

"Just touch me," her mouth begged against his, "hold me." She felt his arms tighten and reveled in his strength. "Love me," her dark eyes pleaded for what only he could give.

Bram tumbled her pliant form backward into the cushions, his body trembling with urgent need as he stripped away the last vestiges of clothing that impeded their union.

The hard weight that impressed Roxanne only amplified her arousal as did the featherlike kisses that were rained on her face, shoulders, and breasts. "Bram, please . . ." Her hands slid down his back, followed his spine, and goaded his sinewy buttocks with provocative pressure.

His hand slid down her flat stomach, a gentle

finger caressing the warm, moist center of her femininity. Feverish tremors wracked her body, and she heard him sigh in satisfaction to her own gratification. Her senses alive with a brilliant burning, Roxanne was stunned to find she begged for possession. "I want you." Her voice was thick with desire. "Oh, Bram, please make love to me now."

"Now is just the beginning of forever," came Bram's rasping vow. Pausing, she heard the rustle of the foil packet just a second, his face filling her eyes. "I love you." Then slowly, carefully, he merged with her body, the sensual pleasure so intense that they both gasped in unison.

Roxanne was flooded with contentment and closeness. It was as if she disappeared into him completely, bodies and souls merging on many dimensional planes, each wrapped in the perfection of themselves and in each other—two becoming as one.

For a timeless moment Bram savored the wonder of this first intimate joining, and then he began to move, setting a tender but forceful silken rhythm that enticed Roxanne's mutual response.

She gripped the unyielding muscles of his shoulders, letting his strength anchor her to reality while her body and mind spiraled into a universe she had never dreamed existed. A sharp cry escaped her, her teeth sinking a not-too-gentle love bite into Bram's perspiration-damp flesh as she became constricted by exquisite, pulsating sensations.

His arms and hands tightened around her, pressing her closer as his body surged and burst in final violence before collapsing in pleasure. Bram kissed her gently before moving his heavy frame off her.

Noticing the radium dial on his watch, Bram smiled as he lay back next to Roxanne. "Now it's official."

"What's official?" Her satiated body snuggled close, her hands regaining their possessive hold on his waist.

"The New Year." His fingers played amid her damp curls. "Happy New Year, love."

A sleepy yawn escaped her. "You already said that an hour ago."

"That was New Year in the Eastern time zone." His foot kicked up the drapery quilt; he caught the edge and wrapped it around them. "Now it's midnight here."

"Hmm . . . you made good your threat." Roxanne raised her head and studied his smiling features in the flickering shadows. "You did say you were going to make love to me before the New Year dawns."

"So I did."

She gave him a light kiss and settled against his side. "And very well too."

CHAPTER EIGHT

Roxanne's nose suddenly twitched in appreciation. "What a wonderful dream! I smell hot coffee."

"Very hot," agreed a cheerful masculine voice.

Half-hooded, sleepy brown eyes blinked Bram's smiling face into focus. "You broke into the machine and heated the coffee over a candle. Now, that's what I call a full-service banker!" Her index finger dived into the cup, only to be jerked out with an "Ouch!"

Bram caught her hand to his mouth and swiftly kissed the pain away. "I did warn you." He gently sucked the tip of her finger. "You taste good." Safely relocating the cup on his desk, he again took up residency on the floor cushions. "Good morning." His fingers combed and fluffed tousled golden-brown curls.

"Good morning yourself." Her arms looped around his neck as her body stretched itself awake, her lush feminine amplitude conforming tightly to his athletic contours. "And where did you get the hot coffee?"

"The power came back on at three this morning," he explained, his fingers teasing only a little while they stroked her slender back. "Don't you remember the flood of lights?"

"No."

"Me getting up?"

"No."

"All the hammering in the lounge?"

"No."

"And what you did to me when I came back to bed?"

"Nooooo . . . ohhhhh." Roxanne balanced herself on her left elbow, deliberately letting her full breasts tickle against the dark pelt that covered his torso. "Are you sure it was me?" Wide, guileless eyes belied an inner flow of sweet sensations that were making her toes curl.

"Positive." His skilled thumb and forefinger began massaging the slumbering nipple to pert wakefulness. "Hmmm, that's the same reaction as last time. It had to be you." Bram's low-pitched voice caressed her. "You're a heady mixture, fair Roxanne, satin and silk"—his hand took full possession of her breast, rejoicing in the velvety skin—"that suddenly and quite deliciously detonates."

Her knuckles traveled from his cheekbone to the curve of his jaw, the dark morning stubble from his beard oddly provocative as it pricked her hand. "And what happens when I detonate?" Roxanne inquired, her gleaming eyes busily devouring the planes and angles that made his face so wonderfully exciting.

"You make soft little sighs of pleasure in my ear, your entire body tightens around me, and then you begin to shiver ever so sweetly."

"I did all that while I was asleep?" Her head lowered with each word until her lips moved softly on his. "Amazing."

Bram smiled. "No, that's what you kept telling me." Desire made his smile fade. His hand roughly pressed her head down; his mouth, compelling and purposeful, secured custody of her kisses.

Roxanne responded freely; giving of herself, her confidence, and her trust in this man only deepened her ardor. Bram Tyler had a very strange effect on her body, mind, and heart—everything seemed to be in sync, and she discovered a joy in her own sexuality as never before.

Here in this private universe she had undergone a change. A change that alternately frightened and pleased her. But right now, right this moment, Roxanne focused only on the pleasure of being with this man, in this place, at this time.

"You were thinking again," he scolded softly. "Thinking and going far away from me."

She shook her head. "No. I was thinking about coming even closer," her husky voice excited his ear. "I was thinking about doing this . . ." Even white teeth wiggled over his earlobe. "And this . . ." Her tongue lingeringly stalked the cord of his neck, across his chest to tease the tough nipple nearly hidden under black curls. "I was thinking how hungry I am . . ." The black pupils of her eyes mastered the brown irises. "But not for food. Just for you."

He growled with delight. "Do you know what you're doing to me?"

Her hand splayed over his heart. "I can feel what I'm doing to you here and—" The rugged contours of his body lured her hand to further explore, her fingernails dancing an excited rhythm over his heated flesh. She moved from chest to stomach to hip, venturing lower, tormenting the sensitive skin on his inner thigh until at last caressing the very essence of his maleness. "And I can see what I'm doing here."

The longer Roxanne stroked and teased him with hands and words, the more intense her own passion. His gentle coaxing and praising fueled her arousal until she felt ready to explode. "I—I really think you should put on . . ."

"Not yet, love, not yet." Bram took control, hovering over her, his cobalt eyes caressing her flushed features. "I've a hunger too, a hunger only you can appease." He kissed her deeply, savoring the sweetness of her lips.

He peppered her body with hot, urgent kisses. His hands caressed a swollen breast, his mouth homing in on its taut crest, tenderly sucking. An ecstatic whimper fled her throat at the feelings that raced through her body. Heat flooded every pore. She rejoiced at the tender ache Bram was creating, knowing that he would ultimately satisfy her building need.

"Bram, please . . ."

"Shh . . ." His lips played with hers. "Not yet . . ." He filled the tiny cleft in her chin with kisses. "I need this too." His fingers, mouth, and tongue

150

located and probed all the erotic little pockets that made her cry with pleasure. He kept bringing her closer and closer to the precipice, until at last he could deny neither of them the joy of their union.

Roxanne knew utter fulfillment the instant she felt him inside her. Locked in each other's arms, they savored every delicate stroke, relished in the quality of each other. An illusion of unity, but the sensations of love remained their own.

"This is the way I want us to be." Bram's voice was a labored breath in her ear. "Together always." He felt her shudder and then knew his own release. "Forever, love, forever." He placed a tender kiss against her mouth, loath to break their intimate connection but conscious that it must be done.

When Bram returned to his office he was fully dressed and carrying a fresh cup of coffee. He found Roxanne staring out the window. "What's so interesting?" Moving to her side, he placed the cup between her hands and took over fastening the buttons on her shirt.

"No snow." She placed a window-chilled palm against his freshly shaven cheek. "Cold, but no blizzard. I think I hear the groaning and grunting of the plows and sanders."

He scowled at her obvious elation. "You don't have to sound so pleased and excited; I'm enjoying life here at the Hepworth Hilton."

Roxanne wrinkled her nose. "Oh, you! I'm thinking about soaking for hours in a hot, bubble-filled tub and eating something that costs more than a quarter, isn't served in Styrofoam and doesn't fall into a metal bin." She looked at the coffee, grimaced, and put the cup on the window seat.

"Besides, tomorrow's a work day for me. I have a very important appointment. I'm not on vacation and—" Her breath caught; her brown eyes grew wide. "Bram, we've got to get out of here!" Roxanne made a series of erratic movements that got her no-where. "This bank reopens at nine tomorrow morn-ing! How would it look if they found their new seventh vice president had been shacked up with a ⊤ . . . a belly-gram for three days!"

"Shacked up!" His large hands roughly clamped against her upper arms. "Shacked up!" Bram's voice was unnaturally high. "That's not you, that's not me, that's not what happened."

She blinked at the harshness that transformed his features. "I—I—" Roxanne stopped stammering and took a deep, calming breath. "I was thinking about you and your reputation and your career." She twisted free. "Something you've obviously forgot-ten."

"It seems there's a lot you've forgotten," came his caustic rejoinder. "How about last night and early this morning and just a little while ago?"

Turning away, she pushed shaky fingers through her hair. "I haven't forgotten anything. I'm—I'm just being mature and practical about it."

"It?" Bram pulled her back against his chest. "That's what you call love—an *it*?"

Her eyes focused on the hands that gently stroked her shoulders. "Love?" Her tone was skeptical, her voice tight and strained. "Come on, Abraham Tyler, you don't have to keep up the charade for my benefit. I'm not the type of woman who'll hold you to all those whispered promises."

"How mature and practical of you!"

Roxanne grew defensive. "That's me—mature and practical. You're the blatant romantic," she accused him. "You're the one who's convinced himself that he's in love."

"And you don't think I am?"

"I know *I'm* not!" Thankful that she wasn't looking at him, Roxanne caught her lower lip, wondering why her words sounded less than positive. She strove to enunciate more forcefully. "I didn't promise you anything." Her eyes shifted to the cushioned mattress on the carpet and on the still-visible indentations two bodies had made. "I didn't deceive you."

"Prince Rainier fell in love with Grace Kelly in three days."

The amusement in Bram's voice made Roxanne erupt in anger. "That does it!" She swiveled around and confronted him, her narrowed gaze assaulting his smiling features. "I did not *ask* to have you love me. In fact I do not *want* you to love me. I'm not interested in having any man love me right now."

He chucked her under her chin. "Keep that up and no man will." Bram favored her with another broad smile. "No man but me."

There was no missing the steely undertone of his words or the dangerous glint in his blue eyes. *It's not fair,* she thought, *I'm just not ready for this confrontation. At least not now, not when I get this silly little puddle of warmth forming in my stomach and can still feel how wonderful he felt on top of me.*

"Let—let's get this place picked up." Roxanne grabbed the empty corn chip bag and two candy wrappers off his desk blotter. "Come on." Her elbow angled a sharp jab into his side. "You know how *tidy* I am."

Dusting and scrubbing and vacuuming were absolutes—a physical effort that yielded visible results. Just the inroad into reality that made Roxanne start thinking again. Thinking that made her extremely irritable, defensive, and anxious.

She pushed the cleaning crew's cart back into the closet marked JANITOR and returned to the lounge to inspect her labors. "I don't believe it!" She lifted a rumpled pile of magazines from the floor and accused Bram. "I just got through straightening this place up, Mr. Tyler. Honestly, Bram, how could you create more garbage?"

"It was simple." He flashed her an engaging grin.

"Don't look so pleased with yourself," came her sarcastic retort as she dumped the stack of magazines into the metal waste can. "And if you've been doing the same in the other rooms, go clean them up."

He sidled next to her and snaked an arm around her waist. "I'd rather do something else." He nuzzled the sensitive skin below her ear.

"I'm sure you would, but you're not going to." Roxanne's icy tone belied a steadily increasing pulse rate. She yelped when he teasingly branded her neck with a love bite and hastily skittered around the table. "We are not amused."

"I find you wittily seductive in spite of your Victorian manners," Bram complimented her with all the Cary Grant-ish charm he could muster. "Come on, Roxy, lighten up. I bet even Aunt Mathilda is on my side in this." He trailed after her until the ladies' room door was rudely slammed in his face.

By three o'clock Roxanne had the fourth floor of the Hepworth National Bank gleaming as no cleaning crew had ever left it. She handed Bram the collection of toiletries he had loaned her. "That's the last of it. No one would guess anyone's been here all this time." Three vertical lines marred her usually smooth forehead. "Although there are the slightly brutalized vending machines," Roxanne sighed. "I'll leave that explanation for you. You were the last one in the bank on Friday."

"Gee, thanks." Rocking back in his executive chair, Bram scrutinized her disposition. "What now?"

"Well . . ." She cleared her throat. "I'm going to put on my coat and boots, take the skyway to the center of the city, and have a cab take me home."

"What about me?"

"You?" Roxanne frowned and dragged a finger across the lemon-oiled oak desktop. "You, why you'll take a cab to the airport and wait for the plane to St. Croix."

Bram favored her with a nasty smile. "My, my, but you are a good little tidier. Have all your other affairs been tidied this neatly?"

"I've never had an affair that needed to be tidied!" She bristled. "And . . . and I'm not sure this"—

155

Roxanne's hand made a wavy gesture—"this . . . what we had was an affair . . . and . . . and I see how quickly you've turned your declaration of love into an affair," she brazened just as nastily.

His white teeth flashed. "Bothers you, does it?"

Roxanne drew herself to her full height. "Nothing about *you* bothers me. Nothing about this weekend bothers me."

"Bravo!" He clapped his hands. "But you're lying." His hands sliding around the back of his head, Bram relaxed into the brown leather cushion. "I can tell you're lying. I know more about you than—"

"Oh, really." Her left shoulder lifted in disdain. "I see you're back to using that wonderful *minor* in psychology again. Since you know me so well, I'm sure you'll know exactly what I'm going to do next." With that, Roxanne turned and stalked out of his office to the lounge.

"You're not going anywhere," he caroled. "You're bluffing."

"You accused me of that once before." She yelled back as she jammed sock-covered feet into leather boots. "Bluffing, am I?" Roxanne struggled into the still-damp, still-skunk-smelling, raccoon-dyed-to-look-like-fox coat. "The gall of that man! Knows all about me, does he? Huh!" She smashed the fedora onto her head and stomped loudly down the corridor.

Bram caught her at the elevator. "Hey, wait! What the hell are you doing? Where are you going?"

Wrenching her arm free, she pushed the strap on her purse over her shoulder. "Don't you know?"

From beneath the brown felt hat brim her eyes glittered a menacing message. "I thought you knew all about me." Her thumb jabbed the call button, the doors slid open, and she stepped inside. "I thought you knew more about me than I did." Roxanne's fingers wiggled good-bye as the doors slid closed, cutting off Bram's sputtering expletive and astonished expression.

His hand wiped across his mouth and jaw. "Damn it to hell, Tyler, talk about all the stupid moves! The lady wasn't bluffing." Bram's brooding features gradually lightened. "But now it's my deal and"—he rubbed his hands in delicious anticipation—"the dealer gets to choose the game!"

Shoveling snow was a mindless task that made Roxanne inordinately happy. Frowning, she lifted and tossed another heaping shovelful off the concrete drive before correcting herself—she was not happy, she was just one step closer to complete exhaustion. And that state had definite appeal.

Good, hard, back-breaking labor. The perfect prescription. She rolled her shoulders and stretched the aching muscles for a moment before continuing. Roxanne took all her aggressions out on the snow, fiercely attacking and pounding and chopping it with the metal shovel. "Someone should have done this to me," she hissed. "Someone should have smacked some sense into me three days ago."

A stitch in her side nearly doubled her over. Roxanne stopped and inhaled two lungfuls of frigid air, then reached into the zippered pocket of her cranberry parka for a tissue to wipe her frozen nose. Nose! That made her think of Bram.

Roxanne sniffed and reattacked the hard-packed, icy mountain at the end of her driveway with renewed vigor. "What I wouldn't give for a time machine." The steel blade chipped away at what the city snowplows left. "Seventy-two hours ago Abraham Tyler and his nose hadn't stuck their way into my nice, tidy life. Tidy!" She growled the word. "I can be just as messy as the next person!"

Her oversize snowmobile boots worked with the shovel to kick, stomp, and break open a path wide enough for a car to enter the drive. She looked at her efforts and saw herself. "What a mess! What an absolutely stupid thing to have done."

She collapsed into the fifty-three new inches of freshly fallen snow and wondered what had come over her. She had never had, never even fantasized about having, a quick sexual encounter in her life. And yet, that's exactly what she had done! "Slam-bam-thank-you-sir!" she cackled at the overcast sky.

Maybe it was her age. She'd read in an article that women don't reach their prime until their thirties and she was going to be thirty-one on the last day of August. Maybe all her hormones were going out of whack. Maybe she had suffered a mutant inner sexual collision that would never be repeated.

Roxanne's arms and legs made scissor motions in the snow, creating a perfect angel. She stood up carefully, looked down at the image, snickered, and fell backward into another high bank. She continued to lay on the icy mattress, her thoughts rambling along a myriad of roads that led to nowhere.

She was concerned about herself, troubled about losing her self-respect, fearful of how much she had changed, and even more confused about the man who had wrought all these changes. What made Abraham Tyler more desirable than any other man she had met? What made him more instantly provocative than even her former fiancé?

Her personal life, Roxanne readily admitted, had TIDY stamped all over it. To her, love and marriage was an eternal commitment. She had thought she was in love with Robert and had been very sensible about their physical relationship. When their engagement had ended, the loss of her beliefs was more a catastrophe than the loss of the man.

That time her principles had failed her; this time she had failed her principles. Wasn't love supposed to be entered into calmly and sensibly and rationally? It certainly couldn't be this—Roxanne swallowed—this all-encompassing fire that devoured her the instant Abraham Tyler even looked at her, let alone touched her.

Bram's touch. The memory of it flooded her veins and warmed her despite her frozen surroundings. His well-shaped mouth was warm and wonderfully sensual. His hands and fingers could inflict the most wildly thrilling sensations.

Roxanne relived the tenderness yet toughness of his firm flesh that moved so provocatively across her heated skin. Inside her leather-palmed wool gloves, her fingers wiggled in remembrance of Bram's sinewy strength. She had reveled in the different textures that mapped his virile body, delighted in discovering all his secret little erogenous zones, and was intoxicated by the fact that her hands, her mouth, her body, could make him tremble and writhe with the same overwhelming ecstasy that he bestowed on her.

Her tongue slowly circled ChapStick-coated lips but tasted the salty dampness that had slicked Bram's shoulder. She recalled how perfectly her chin had fit into that particular masculine hollow, how her tongue had drawn teasing little circles along the bone and up the cord of his neck and had played with his earlobe.

Gradually Roxanne became aware of the fact that she was unbelievably hot and her body was melting a duplicate of itself into the ice-coated snow. "Great, just great! Even when he's not with me he can still set me burning!" Gloved fists created an avalanche that enveloped her from waist to knees.

"What am I going to do?" To her own ears her voice sounded weak and scared. "Hell, haven't I done enough!" She piled more snow on herself. "Female entrepreneur found frozen on front lawn. Film at eleven." What a lovely headline for the TV news and the perfect answer!

Her irrational mumblings were abruptly and loudly interrupted by a car horn. Roxanne sat up and blinked questioningly at the navy Nissan that slowly crept along the driveway to stop at the door of the garage. While the car was a stranger, the occupant wasn't. She scurried to her feet and stared in amazement at the six-foot-two, black-haired, blue-eyed, broad-shouldered male holding a suitcase. "Abraham Tyler, what are you doing here?"

Bram reached around and brushed the snow off the seat of her ski pants with possessive familiarity. "I'm here for a vacation."

CHAPTER NINE

"Vacation!" Roxanne squeaked in the most undignified of tones. "What do you mean, vacation? Here? Vaca—"

Bram merely smiled, ignored her agitation, and looked over her shoulder at the house. "So this is stately Murdoch Manor. Ah, I see I was right." Skirting her puffing figure, he proceeded up the walk, talking as he inspected the Christmas-lit dwelling. "Pre–World War II red brick bungalow. Well-constructed and well-kept in a long-established neighborhood of equally well-preserved homes that exudes a certain intimacy about life in this community."

She rolled her eyes and trudged after him, boots creaking along the hard-packed snow. "Are you leaving banking and going into real estate?"

He took a deep breath. "Hmmm . . . just smell that air. I've always loved the way wood smoke softens the crispness." His fingers stroked the red and green velvet ribbon on the pine-cone door wreath. "Nice."

Bram opened the outer storm door and, despite

Roxanne's sputtering, ventured inside. "Very nice . . . a touch of spring in Siberia. *Yellow* cushions on the pipe furniture." His tongue clicked against the roof of his mouth. "Roxy, I thought you hated yellow."

Easing his snow-dampened shoes off, Bram placed them on the boot tray, stockinged feet wiggling against the rough green Astro turf that served as a rug. "How efficient of you to seal these windows with heavy-duty plastic." Dark eyebrows lifted suddenly. "Did you say something?"

"Just a word I once read on a bathroom wall!" Roxanne seethed, and then smiled sweetly. "Okay, Abraham Tyler, what's going on? Just what do you think you're doing?"

"You know, I was just going to ask you the same question. What were you doing lying in a rather erotic spread-eagle in the snow?"

"I was designing a snow-gram," she wisecracked, bending to unfasten the buckles on her boots.

"Ahh." He looked back out the window. "You've really accomplished a lot in the last three hours twelve minutes and—" Bram consulted his watch. "Forty-one seconds. Did you have any trouble getting home?"

"For the cab fare I paid I should be sunning myself in Palm Beach," Roxanne announced. Hands on hips, she looked him up and down. "Speaking of warm sunny climates, why aren't you in St. Croix watching the bikinis go by?"

"Because you're not in one," came his easy response. Bram's right hand caressed her ice-pinked cheek. "Are you all right? Was your house okay?"

The warmth of his hand and the gentleness in his voice assaulted Roxanne's tightly leashed emotions and splintered them into thousands of quicksilver pieces that made her prickle with feminine awareness. She swallowed hard. "I . . . I'm fine." Her eyes were held prisoner by his, and if she let the truth be known, she didn't want to escape.

Minute by minute she was discovering an inner contentment and bliss in the silly madness Bram Tyler could create. "The—the clocks were only off a few hours, no pipes froze, and the freezer didn't defrost. I—I called my parents, pulled on my ski clothes, and along with everyone else started shoveling. . . ."

Roxanne stopped babbling when she saw his mouth curve in the most appealing smile. "Bram, why are you here?"

"Because I love you." Quickly he removed his hand from her face and proceeded to open the front door of the house. "Would you like to know what I've been doing for the last three hours"—he inspected his watch again—"twenty minutes and twelve seconds?" Upon hearing Roxanne's lengthy sigh, he blithely continued. "I walked back to where I left the car on Friday, found a tow truck in search of abandoned vehicles, and made a nice deal that included repairs and a lift to the airport. I then rented that sporty little import, reclaimed my luggage, drove home, showered, changed, and came here"—Bram

164

patted the brown soft-sided carry-all—"all repacked for a chilly climate."

"The one inside or the one outside?" Roxanne parried and then grew serious. "Look, you just can't . . . can't vacation here, in my house. It's . . . it's . . ."

"Crazy? Insane? Undignified?" He was quick to supply some appropriate words. "Weren't you the one who said I needed to be more of the above. Say, Murdoch Manor is quite charming." Bram grinned at her. "And you're right, not a doily in sight."

Roxanne opened her mouth and screamed.

"Hey!" His palm clamped tightly against her lips. "Are you crazy! Your neighbors will think you're being attacked."

She yanked away his hand. "Good. I hope they call the police and—"

"The police are very reluctant to involve themselves in domestic disputes."

"We are not in a domestic situation!" Fascinated by his carefree manner, Roxanne gauged Bram's every move. He placed his suitcase on her gray and peach-toned sculptured carpet, removed his heavy sheepskin jacket and hung it on the Victorian hall-tree, calmly settled himself in the brown suede rocker-recliner that was angled toward the fireplace, and reached for the poker to jab the low-flaming logs into a more vivid, productive display.

Damn the man! She silently fumed. *He certainly gives the impression he's in a domestic situation. He acts like he owns this place, owns me. Hell, he's even taken over the ownership of my favorite chair!*

Viciously Roxanne pulled open the zipper of her parka, fought her way out of the quilted nylon sleeves, jammed it on the halltree peg, and then followed suit with sodden ski pants. She clenched shaky hands into tight fists, shook back perspiration- and snow-dampened curls, and headed to do battle. "Now, you look here, Bram, you just can't commandeer my home, you—"

"Why?"

She blanched. "What do you mean why? Why . . . why . . . wh—"

"I see you're still wearing my shirt and socks." He tugged the shirttail hem, his fingers lightly grazing her sleek thigh. "You really do something for men's clothes, Roxy."

The second she felt his touch on her skin Roxanne knew she should have taken one step back. She knew she should, but she didn't; she couldn't, she wouldn't. And when he took his hand away, she felt resentful. "I—I told you I just grabbed on heavier clothes and started to dig out." Then she added loftily, "I couldn't take the time to shower and change."

"Have you had dinner?"

"Dinner?" came her confused echo.

"Hmmm."

Brown eyes narrowed. "Listen, if you think I'm going to be your damn maid and wait on you hand and foot—"

"I'll make dinner." Bram smiled and stood up. "I'm sure after all your snow-shoveling and snow-graming you'd welcome a long soak in a bubble-filled tub and then wrapping yourself in that fluffy blue

166

bathrobe you mentioned." He fingered the very tips of the shirt collar, his knuckles stroking the sharp edge of the striped cotton. "Go on, Roxy, I'll find my way to the kitchen, and then after I've fed you and your civility has returned, we can talk."

Roxanne's shoulders slumped, she issued a resigned sigh followed by a confused collection of mumbled words, and then wandered down the short hallway, past the adjoining dining room, into the safer, much saner haven of the bathroom.

She couldn't have been submerged in the tub for more than five minutes when a knock rattled the door. "Ahhh, I knew it." Her voice was low and predatory. "He was just waiting for me to get my clothes off and then—" Her hand clawed at the frothing white bubbles. "What?" Roxanne snapped.

"Are you decent?"

"I was until last Friday," she shot back and then sank lower into the steaming, scented water as Bram eased his way into the pale blue and white bathroom.

He pulled a thick white towel from the bar, tossed it on the floor by the tub, and settled himself Indian-style. "You don't think you're decent anymore?"

His earnest inquiry demanded a serious response. Roxanne decided to tell Bram exactly how she felt. "No, I'm not sure I am decent. Decency is conforming to recognized standards of propriety and morality, and what proper, moral, decent woman ends up making love to a man she's met only two days before?"

"You did."

She frowned and watched her wet fingers squeak

167

across the blue enamel tub rim. "I've never done that before. I didn't think I could." Troubled brown eyes studied his relaxed features. "I don't know why I did."

"I do." Bram covered her wet hand with his. "And so do you, you just said it." He smiled at her confusion and explained, "You made love not sex."

Roxanne wiggled free of his grasp. "That . . . that was just one of those polite little euphemisms," she stammered. "I was trying to be civil."

"I like you better when you're more yourself—unpretentious and wholesomely earthy." Bram reached into the tub and scooped up a handful of iridescent suds. "You know, at one point this past weekend I was overcome by a surprise attack of primitive jealousy over your ex-fiancé, but now I realize he never touched the real Roxanne Murdoch." His gaze shifted from inspecting the bubbles to focus on her face. "But I did. I'm the lucky one. I touched her, tasted her, loved her, pleasured her, and she did the same to me and did it quite freely and willingly and very wonderfully."

Her breath caught. "Oh, so that's why you're here. You . . . you think you can just . . . just continue to use my body freely and willingly and . . . and . . ."

"I'm not interested in your body."

She blinked. "You're—you're not?"

Bram was having a hard time swallowing the laughter that formed from hearing her disappointed tone. "Nope." He let what was left of the bubbles in his hand float back into the silken water, his fingers

168

fluttering lightly before he removed and dried his hand. "I better get started on that dinner I promised you. Don't stay too long." He stood up and headed for the door. "Omelets begin to lose their culinary appeal after twenty minutes."

The waves Bram had instigated in the bath water washed like a warm, slow tide against Roxanne. Her breasts responded to the infinite caresses with the same eager anticipation they gave to the man who created the whirlpool. Anticipation that went unrequited immediately transformed itself into the most uncomfortable ache.

Emitting a groan that sounded more like a sob, she turned on the water faucet, stood up, pulled the knob for the shower release, and directed an icy spray over her heated body.

"You do make a delicious omelet," Roxanne grudgingly extended the compliment. "Thank you." She curved slightly shaky hands around a nearly filled mug of orange spice tea. "With all the snow-shoveling I did, I'm not even sure I would have had the strength to do more than climb into a nice warm bed and fall asleep."

"I'm looking forward to falling asleep next to you."

Her eyes widened, then narrowed suspiciously. "I thought you said you weren't interested in my body."

An enigmatic expression curtained his rough-hewn features. "I'm not. I just know that I won't be able to sleep unless you're curled next to me." He began to clear the plates and utensils off the round

169

maple captain's table, and rinse them in the stainless steel sink before stacking them into the dishwasher.

"My mother used to have an embroidered plaque in our kitchen that read 'A house is built of brick and stone; a home is built of love alone,' " Bram rambled, shaking detergent into the cup in the dishwasher's door, closing and locking it and throwing the switch. "That's what I saw here as I explored your home."

"Thank you very much." She fiddled with the zipper pull on the front of her blue robe. "I've done the decorating myself, coordinating it with the few antiques my aunt had that I was pleased with." Roxanne discovered even more pleasure in her accomplishments after hearing Bram's compliments.

He took a sponge and wiped the top of the avocado-toned stove. "Aunt Mathilda's bedroom was just as you described—a massive waterbed and pink-plumed fans that match the walls and carpet."

Roxanne smiled at him. "I didn't have the heart to touch that room. It's not a shrine but . . ." Her voice trailed off.

"It's just Mathilda," Bram finished, and watched her nod in agreement. "Are there any scrapbooks or other mementoes? I want to meet this lady."

"In her room, on the shelf under the night table." Roxanne then patted back a series of yawns. "Just looking at the changes in photo processing is a history lesson." Another wide yawn was issued. Roxanne shook her head. "I'm sorry. I think old Morpheus is creeping up on me."

"Time for bed. After all, you have to work tomorrow."

She watched Bram's arms encircle her waist and savored the virile strength in him that allowed him so easily to sweep her off the chair and carry her down the short hallway. It was an intoxicating experience that overwhelmed her sensibilities. No man had ever carried her anyplace!

Bram's elbow hit the light switch and the apricot-toned decor blossomed into pastel ripeness. "This room is you, Roxy." He gently sat her on the edge of the flower-decorated satin quilt that covered the double-size brass bed. "A wonderful mix of textures and patterns tempered by a sophisticated, yet unspoiled color."

"Sophisticated? No, I'm not blasé enough about things." She shrugged off her robe. "Bram, you're not really going to sleep in here, are you?"

"Yup." He consulted his watch. "But not right now. It's only nine thirty." His smile was easy. "I'm going to find a book to read in that nice little den you've made in the third bedroom, maybe watch a little TV." Bram shooed her under the covers and tucked them tightly under the mattress. "I'll make sure the fire screen is in place and turn off the outdoor lights. I want to check your Christmas tree; it looks like it needs water."

She yawned and had trouble keeping her eyes opened. "It's artificial."

"Hmmm, they certainly make them look real!" He reached down and curved his hand against the side of her face, his palm cupping a softly blushed cheek, fingers relishing the embrace of silken curls. "Goodnight, love."

* * *

Roxanne was forced to check the security of the gold hoops in her ears with her fingers because her eyes refused to focus on her mirror image, concentrating instead on the reflection of the sleep-tousled bed. There was no doubting Bram had slept there. The white pillowcase beside her showed his head's impression and the sheets were still warm from his body, bearing a telltale trace of his musky cologne.

But when the alarm went off at seven, the man himself had been missing. Roxanne heard him in the kitchen conducting a rather noisy concert with pans, dishes, cups, and silverware. That's where he had stayed, leaving the bathroom and the bedroom completely free for her use.

She pulled open a dresser drawer, hunting for a brown leather belt and a pastel-striped scarf to tuck in the rounded neckline of her blue wool suit jacket. The scarf was an easy discovery; the belt she finally located peeking out from under Bram's suitcase that was balanced on the bedroom chair.

He was living out of that bag, his clothes neatly piled according to function: underwear, handkerchiefs, turtleneck sweaters, two plaid shirts, jeans, and two pair of winter-weight slacks. A heavy black velour knee-length kimono-style robe was thrown over the chair's ladderback, but no pajamas were in evidence.

Roxanne shivered despite the solid warmth in the room. How could she have slept next to a naked man and not known it? Especially when that naked man was Abraham Tyler. "Abraham." Her husky voice tenderly spoke his name, taking time to caress each syllable, wishing she was caressing and stroking the man, wishing he was caressing and stroking her.

The hand that had mesmerized her, the hand that was fondling the belt on his robe, now reached up to smartly slap her cheek. "Thanks, I needed that!" Roxanne took a deep breath, masked her features in a well-practiced professional veneer, and headed for the kitchen.

"Good morning. You look bright-eyed and well-rested." He slid a dish of buttered toast onto the table. "Any effects from all the shoveling?"

She swallowed a mouthful of orange juice. "No, I'm used to it." Her eyes lingered longer than was necessary on his back, finding pleasure in the rippling muscles that were defined beneath his smoothly fitting camel sweater and tucked into tan corduroys. "I'm not one for a big breakfast."

"I remember." Bram pulled out her chair. "Just juice, toast, and coffee." He reached for the steaming carafe and filled her cup. "You're welcome to use the rental car to get to work; I know yours is still at the garage."

"Thanks, but I carpool with my neighbor across the street," Roxanne explained. "Charlie works in the office next to mine in the La Salle Building, so we alternate driving and split parking fees." She added sugar and cream to the aromatic brew. "I'll bring my car home tonight and—"

"What's the matter?" He looked up from spreading raspberry jam on his toast.

173

"I . . . I just remembered, I have a business dinner meeting tonight."

"Fine, but thanks for telling me. I was going to wow you with my famous chicken and noodle casserole, but I'll save it for tomorrow—" He hesitated. "If your schedule permits."

Roxanne noticed there was no sarcasm in Bram's tone, only interest, and she found herself launching into detail about her appointment. "I think I mentioned that I was considering franchising Greetings and Salutations, plus I have an idea for expansion."

"Tell me."

"Well . . ." She hesitated for a moment, and then explained. "I've been creating telephone-answering tapes for businesses that can be used to recite hours, advertising specials, giving alternative names and numbers—things like that. Each would be designed for a specific company, no two alike." She leaned back and waited for his reaction.

"That is a stroke of brilliance," Bram decreed. "I must admit my pet peeve is the recorded message, but your idea transcends that by saving my time and money with information." He refilled the stoneware coffee mug. "This meeting tonight, will it help get your project off the ground?"

She shrugged. "That I don't know. I've never met Emmett Lewis in person, only through letters and speaking over the phone. He likes my ideas and I like the fact he wants to be a silent partner, but I want to meet him and sound him out on a few more questions and policies."

"You have a gifted business acumen, Roxy. I have no doubt you'll make the right decision."

She felt her cheeks warm at his flattery. "What—what are you going to do today?"

Bram folded his paper napkin into a fan. "Oh, I thought I'd do some more reading. You have a nice collection of mystery and detective novels that intrigue me, and maybe"—he smiled at her—"I'll dust the cobwebs off your dining room chandelier."

Her eyebrow lifted. "Do you do windows too?"

"I do lots of things," came his easy drawl. "Remember?"

Roxanne had an extremely difficult time breaking his mesmerizing gaze. "I—I think I hear Charlie's car horn." Her chair made a rude scraping noise as it slid across the white linoleum. "Well, have a nice day." Such an inane comment, but it was all she could manage as she finished fastening the double row of buttons on her tan steamer coat and slid her stockinged feet into brown leather boots.

"Here's luck for your meeting."

She expected a kiss but received a simple victory sign. *Hardly the loving sendoff,* came Roxanne's silent grumble as she half walked, half skidded down the front walk to the waiting car.

Bram stood in the open front door, watching until the white vapors from the tailpipe condensed into the frigid winter air. The only plan he had for today was sleep—the one item that had been left off last night's menu.

He returned to Roxanne's bedroom and her bed, choosing to sleep on the left side, her side, the satin quilt pulled up over his clothes, tucked tightly under his chin. The slick fabric embraced her scent. Subtle nuances of jasmine and roses tormented his mind and body as did the memory of sleeping next to her, lying so close, yet not being able to touch.

A reminiscent smile curved Bram's lips. Whoever said flannel nightgowns were unflattering and sexless would change their mind when they saw Roxanne in her pink and white striped ankle-length gown. Despite the voluminous fabric and convent styling, the brushed cotton had conformed to her full breasts and molded the contours of her long legs.

The view had been sexy and inviting, as provocative this morning as it had been at eleven thirty last night, and the resulting hardness that taunted Bram's muscles hadn't diminished in the ensuing nine hours. He rolled on his side, bunching the pillows under his head, and mumbled, "I don't know how long I can keep this up!"

Little things began to play on his memory: the way she licked the butter off her fingers at breakfast, the glimpse of a sleek, stockinged thigh as she lifted her blue skirt to slide her foot into her boot, the way the kitchen fluorescent light played shimmering games on her hair.

"Hell!" The word came out a groan. "Maybe I shouldn't keep acting so indifferently. Maybe I should just attack." Bram pulled the cover over his head and struggled his way toward sleep.

It was nearly midnight when Roxanne returned

home. She found Bram in bed with Agatha Christie. "Miss Marple?"

He grinned. "I keep thinking Aunt Mathilda could have done a nice job playing her on the screen."

Roxanne sighed and sat on the end of the mattress. "I should have stayed home with you and formed a menage à trois with Miss Marple."

Bram put the paperback facedown on the night table. "What went wrong, Roxy, dinner or the meeting?"

"The chef at IDS's Orion Room couldn't make a bad meal." Beneath the covers she felt his feet wiggle against her thigh. Roxanne turned a sorrowful expression toward him. "Emmett should be renamed weasel; he tried to turn a business meeting into a tête-à-tête."

"Oh. What happened?"

The gruffness in his voice warmed her. "I don't really know," Roxanne admitted, unbuckling her belt and tugging the scarf free of her neckline. "Emmett Lewis was not like his letters. He didn't take me or my company or my new project seriously." She stood up and moved to open the louvered closet doors, unbuttoning her jacket and skirt along the way.

"I tried to acquaint him with the fact the idea for Greetings and Salutations actually dated back to 1933, when the first singing telegram was issued. Our special delivery messages were more like miniature Broadway shows-to-go, all in good fun and certainly more memorable than any card or gift." She slid off

177

her wool jacket, stepped out of the matching skirt, and reached for the appropriate hangers.

Clad only in a black full slip, Roxanne turned. "When I applied for the loan at your bank, you treated me as a professional; you didn't make any snickering, tawdry comments." Her hand thumped just above her breast. "I think I give a competent business presentation."

"I know you do," Bram agreed. With mounting fascination he watched Roxanne's graceful strip-tease. She was totally oblivious to the ease in which she was undressing in front of him.

She sighed and shook her head. "Damn, I wish you had been there. Lewis was just so slick, so glib, so . . . slimy." She shivered as the satin straps slid down her arms and the slip formed a midnight pud-dle at her feet.

"He had a few X-rated suggestions for messages that he wanted to incorporate in the franchise." Rox-anne wriggled out of her panty hose. "X-rated! I nearly died!" She turned and reached inside the clos-et for her nightgown.

"You're right." Bram fought to control his erratic breathing. "The man is a weasel, and you're well rid of him." His eyes lingeringly caressed her tapered back, velvety buttocks, and slender limbs that tantal-ized and tempted for one heavenly minute before the flannel curtain dropped.

"It's a shame really. He made me a franchise offer of twenty thousand with five percent of revenues." Roxanne climbed between the sheets. "Now I'll have to find someone else with money to invest."

Feeling inordinately happy over her natural reactions, Bram snapped off the light and slipped an arm around her shoulders, drawing her head against his chest. "Roxy, I'm sure you'll be able to find someone who appreciates your business and your ideas. I happen to think you're a very clever, talented person."

"Thanks." Beneath her cheek his firm torso felt warm, vital, and instantly arousing. Roxanne strove to sound normal. "The house looks lovely, all polished and vacuumed, and the chandelier glitters in the dark."

"Thank you, ma'am." His hand made a slow tour of her shoulders, coming to rest on the back of her head. "It was fun, although I was lonely." His fingers swirled amid the soft brown curls. "This was the first day we spent apart and I missed not having you around."

"I—I missed you too," came her honest answer. She slid her legs closer to his, hinting at further intimacy. "It did seem a very long day." Her toes suggestively groped his.

"Oh, honey, what a brute I am." Bram pulled his arms away. "You need sleep, not talk." He edged farther away. "Good night."

Roxanne pouted at the ceiling. *Good night!* She didn't need all that much sleep. Her pout turned into a frown. She didn't want all that much sleep.

What do you want? What do you need? prompted an inner voice. Roxanne turned her head, her eyes sculpting Bram's forehead in the opaque darkness. She needed and wanted Abraham Tyler. She had missed him all day and she had wished for his wise

179

counsel at various times tonight and right now, right this instant, she was wishing for and missing terribly being held in his arms and having him kiss her thoroughly.

Her needs and wants and misses and wishes were the main reason why on Wednesday night, when she came into the bedroom after taking a hot bath, Roxanne was wearing a short silk nightshirt rather than her practical flannel gown.

CHAPTER TEN

Looking over the top of *Murder Most Foul,* Bram's blue eyes widened with interest but blithely returned to the aged Miss Marple until the youthful Miss Murdoch made the first move.

Undaunted, Roxanne tried another provoking tactic. She stood next to the bed, exhaled an exaggerated sigh, languidly stretching her arms so that the teal silk slipped up and down her body.

Without looking up, Bram politely inquired, "Did you say something?"

Her lips thinned. "No." Roxanne decided to stop playing the coquette and proceed with the main assault. She sidled across the lavender sheets. "Bram . . ." she muttered, and plastered her womanly curves along the full length of his lean contours. "How much longer are you going to read?"

"Oh, I'm sorry, honey." He folded down the page corner, dropped the book on the oak night table, and twisted off the light. "Good night, Roxy."

A chill peppered her skin as his warm body turned

away. "Bram . . ." Her husky voice purred into his ear while her hand moved slowly and suggestively down his chest to settle low on his stomach, her pinky making erotic dips and swirls into his navel.

"What the hell do you think you're doing?"

His harsh, rude growl shocked her. "Well, I— I—" Roxanne stuttered her way into inanity. "I—I just thought that we . . . er . . . might . . . uh . . . well . . ."

"You haven't said more than a handful of words to me since you got home from work, and now *this*!" Bram lifted her hand from his hip. "Really, Roxanne! And you had the audacity to accuse me of wanting you for *your* body!" He turned his head. "What am I? Just stud-service for whenever *you* get the urge?"

Roxanne yanked her arm free and sat up. "For heaven's sake, Bram! How dare you make such a crude remark!"

He snapped on the light and leaned back into the bed pillows. "I make it quite easily." Bram strove to keep his features and voice free of emotion. "When I reach for you, it's out of love and respect and devotion. I don't want to assault your body. I want to *love* you, share something special, something almost spiritual. I'm not being propelled by *lust*!"

"Lust!" Roxanne looked over her shoulder and threw him a dirty look. "I am not lusting." She violently enunciated each word.

"Oh, really! Then what were you doing?"

"Well, I . . . uh . . ." Her legs shifted anxiously beneath the quilt. "Bram . . ." Roxanne wiggled back up next to him. Her expression was woeful; her hand stroked his shoulder. "Couldn't we . . . couldn't I just . . . Hey!" She blinked in astonishment as he tossed aside the covers and left the bed. "What are you doing?"

"I'm leaving." He walked to the chair and put on his clothes with the speed of a fireman.

"Leaving?" Her forehead puckered. "Leaving!" She crouched on all fours. "You—you just can't leave in the middle of the night!"

"Who says?"

"I do!" Roxanne surged forcefully to her feet and tried to keep her balance on the foam mattress. "Damn it, I thought you loved me?"

"I do." Bram looked up from tucking his red plaid shirt into his denims. "I feel that together we can get through anything. The good and the bad." With little regard he began to shove clothes into his suitcase. "For richer or poorer." He zipped the bag, placed it on the floor, and sat in the chair to put on his socks and shoes. "Sickness and health. I'm ready to make a lifetime commitment. But each time I say I love you you throw it back at me." He stood up. "How much of that do you expect me to take?"

"Bram!" She bounced to the end of the bed. "Bram, let's talk about this."

He took a deep breath. "I don't think so. I've done all the talking I'm going to do. Believe it or not, I have a very fragile ego at this point, Roxanne. I know I won't be able to take hearing you say no again."

Bram picked up his bag. "I realize now I've been very bull-headed about ignoring your feelings. I love you enough to respect your wishes. The least you can do is respect me enough not to try and use me for your own gratification." He paused in the doorway. "Let me leave with dignity."

"Bram! Abraham Tyler, you come back here!" Roxanne jumped off the bed and ran after him. "Bram, please wait." She grabbed the fleece-edged sleeve of his jacket. "Please."

It took all Bram's inner strength to ignore her pleading voice and teary expression. "I'm sorry, Roxanne. I thought I could love enough for both of us, but I can't." He caught her trembling chin between his thumb and forefinger. "Here's looking at you, kid."

Roxanne found herself attacked by an icy blast of winter air, and then suddenly she was staring at a closed door. "I didn't even get a good-bye kiss!" Her lower lip protruded in a pathetic pout as she walked back into the living room and flung herself facedown on the couch.

"Maybe this is just a nightmare," came her consoling whisper. "Maybe I'm walking, talking, and sniveling in my sleep." But in the still of the night she heard the roar of his car engine followed by the flash of headlights stabbing into the darkness and knew this was no dream but a horrible reality.

Chin balanced on the sofa arm, Roxanne stared into the shadows and tried to reconstruct exactly what had happened, where she had gone wrong. Bram had been right about her being quiet all evening, but that was because she had been thinking about him and herself.

To be quite truthful, she grudgingly amended, her thoughts had been focused on love. In fact, that had been her entire objective for the night—to show Abraham Tyler just how much she loved him. To show him and tell him and make sweet, wonderful, exciting love to him.

"Did the man even stop and think how difficult it might be for me to admit I was wrong? That you *could* fall in love with someone in three days!" Roxanne groaned. "Three days! That's all it took for one Abraham Tyler to completely demolish me, to get under my skin so completely that . . . that . . ." She sighed and forced herself to speak the truth. "He ruined me for loving any man but him!"

"What a cunning devil! He . . ." Her eyebrows pulled together in remembrance. "He did this once before!" Roxanne sat up. "That stinker pulled the same routine on New Year's Eve!" Her fist pummeled the striped cushion. "Advance, dig in, withdrawal, and sudden retreat."

She slammed the cushion again. "What nerve! If he thinks this is going to be a pattern for the rest of our lives, he's crazy!" Roxanne smiled and giggled happily. "Well, maybe he's not so crazy! I'm the one who's crazy. I'm the one sitting here talking to herself."

Her fingers drummed against her thigh. "Maybe Abraham Tyler should begin to talk to himself and worry a little." Roxanne's eyes glowed with unholy delight. "We Celestial Virgins aren't always mature and responsible; sometimes we can be downright devious!"

* * *

Promptly at six P.M. Friday night, exactly one week to the hour she had first met Abraham Tyler, Roxanne rolled down her car window to speak to the security guard at the Hawk Ridge condominium complex in Edina. "Roxanne Murdoch to see Abraham Tyler." She hesitated slightly before adding, "I—I have an anniversary surprise, so please don't announce me."

"Wouldn't matter if I did," the man returned, his gloved fingers checking the roster. "Mr. Tyler's gone."

"Gone!" came her distressed echo. "What do you mean, he's gone? Where did he go?"

The guard leaned closer to her window, anxious to absorb some of the warm air blowing from the car's heater. "Mr. Tyler left on vacation. I've got orders to hold his mail and collect messages. Do you want to leave one?"

"No." Roxanne sniffed and said a polite goodnight. It took her three attempts to negotiate a U-turn that would take her down the tree-lined access road and onto the Interstate.

Gone! Her mind reverberated that word until her body began to shake with the finality of it. "If I hadn't been so damn stubborn; if I hadn't tried to play games; if I had gotten into my car Wednesday night and followed him, told him I loved him, he wouldn't be gone!" Tears dribbled down Roxanne's checks and teased the corner of her mouth. "Bram would be here, with me, right where he belongs."

Twenty minutes later when she pulled into her

186

driveway, Roxanne was seized with another brilliant idea. She'd go to St. Croix and find him. How difficult could it be; the island wasn't all that big!

Hurriedly, Roxanne scrambled out of the car and headed up the walkway toward her house. She'd call the airlines and book the first flight out tomorrow morning. By tomorrow night Abraham Tyler would have no doubts about how much Roxanne Murdoch loved him. How could any man doubt a woman who would fly halfway around the world to say I love you.

She unlocked the porch door, hopped up and down, discarding her snow-rimmed boots, and stumbled her way into the living room. An enormous white box with SPECIAL DELIVERY stenciled on the side stopped Roxanne cold.

"Whaaa . . . wow!" She walked around the six-foot-square package, a happy smile slowly curving her lips. The smile broadened into a grin when she noticed the fire dancing merrily in the hearth and an ice-filled bucket holding a bottle of champagne and two crystal goblets on the oak end table.

Roxanne sat on the sofa, smoothed her fur coat neatly around her, and waited. After a few minutes she heard a knock from inside the box and dutifully shoved aside the red ribbon-strewn top.

"A man could suffocate in here."

Brown eyes looked with benign interest at Abraham Tyler's smiling face before realizing the rest of him was completely naked. "You're not wearing enough to suffocate."

"Noticed, did you?"

She cleared her throat, her eyes dropping below

187

his waist. "It's becoming more and more obvious, actually."

Bram crossed his arms over his chest. "I decided that being the object of your lustful intentions was better than living without you. So here I am." With a sigh his hands dropped to his sides. "Do with me what you will."

"It's no good, Mr. Tyler." Roxanne put the lid back in place.

"Hey!" A moving mass of arms and legs collapsed the fragilely constructed wrapping. Bram pushed away the debris and stood upright on his knees by her side. "What do you mean that's no good?" He grabbed her wrist. "It was good enough twenty-four hours ago."

"It wasn't good enough then either." Her left hand curved around his cheek. "If you just hadn't been so clever, Mr. Tyler, twenty-four hours ago you would have found out that I wasn't just interested in your body." Her other hand wiggled free and splayed across his heaving chest. "Even though it is the most outstanding, most awe-inspiring male body I have ever been privy to."

"Really," he drawled. "In that case, I think I'll use my inspiring, outstanding body to make you tell me more." Bram pushed her backward into the cushions and wedged himself against her. "Are you going to talk, Miss Murdoch?"

"There are other things I'd rather do." Her fingers stopped their exploring where they had the last time, low on his stomach by his navel. "But since you insist on talking . . ." Roxanne let her pert nose caress his.

"I love you, Abraham Tyler, including your modest but virile nose."

His previous bantering voice turned serious. "When did you come to that revelation?"

"New Year's Eve," she confessed. "It just took a little longer for it to sink into my responsible, mature, practical brain." Roxanne kissed his lower lip. "I wasn't looking for you, but you seemed to have found me anyway. I'll admit I was confused and scared and anxious, but I knew I had to have loved you, otherwise absolutely nothing would have happened that night or any other time."

"Nothing?"

"Not a thing."

Bram laughed and hugged her tight. "You see, I was right all along."

She pouted prettily at him. "You don't have to crow so. You were the one who ended up back here tonight," came Roxanne's smug reminder.

"So I did." His lips pressed close to her ear. "But Jenkins, the security officer, called this number a little while ago and said a Miss Murdoch had indeed shown up."

"You rascal!" The arm she had wrapped around his neck tightened. "How could you know I would show up at your place?"

"Your able office assistant, Miss Suzanne Kendall, is just a joy to talk with," he reported with lazy ease. "I told her my problem in dealing with the irritatingly persnickety Miss Murdoch, and she told me that the same Miss Murdoch was unusually frustrated and careless, alternately teary and giggly, and then

Thursday called in to say she was going shopping for lingerie and probably wouldn't be coming in for at least a week."

Roxanne sighed. "I'll have to give Sue a raise."

"Were you bringing all that lingerie with you to my place?"

"All that I was bringing to your place is under this coat."

"Hmmm . . ." Bram released the three buttons and slid his hand inside. "All I feel is you."

Brown eyes smiled into blue. "That's all you were getting. Me. The complete me. The me no one has ever gotten before."

"I can handle that."

"Forever and ever?"

"And beyond," he promised. His mouth merged with hers, ultimately verifying and sealing a promise for a lifetime. "It's been a long time since I kissed you, Roxy." His tongue slid her soft lips apart, eagerly reacquainting itself with the honeyed recesses beyond. "You taste so good."

Both of his hands had found their way inside her coat. "You feel like warm silk." He tenderly cupped her breasts, palms savoring the velvety swells as his fingers provoked the already-hardened nipples.

Roxanne's low moan of satisfaction was transformed into an urgent request. "According to Cosmopolitan's Bedside Astrologer, my favorite romantic rendezvous are in an office." Her hand traveled farther down Bram's pelvis to gently caress and stroke his burgeoning desire. "Which we've already done and on a fur coat in front of a fire

. . ." Her fingernails drew squiggles against his inner thigh. ". . . both of which we happen to have at our disposal."

His hungry mouth lifted from her breast. "Sounds perfect. Let me just . . ."

She stopped him as he attempted to move away. "I went to your place well-prepared for tonight."

Bram pressed a hard kiss against her mouth, then a very delicate one to her pert nipple. "I can't wait to feel you around me."

"Then don't," she pleaded. Her hands cupped his face. "I love you quite terribly, Mr. Tyler."

With a single, breathtaking stroke, Bram merged their bodies into a glorious reunion. "I love you quite profoundly, Miss Murdoch."

In Aunt Mathilda's bedroom the two pink ostrich plume fans fell off the wall in mute approval.

LOOK FOR NEXT MONTH'S
CANDLELIGHT ECSTASY ROMANCES ®